"If you hadn't made such an outrageous bid...where would I be? Not with the most beautiful woman in the room."

She shook her head. "Don't say things like that, Roman. Not when you don't mean them."

She felt the warm weight of his hands on her shoulders when he stopped their dancing to say, "I mean it." Her words vanished. She suspected no one argued with Roman or doubted his word, so she remained silent.

She was out of her depth with a man like Roman. Being around him made her feel stirrings in her belly and her blood zing.

"Good, I'm glad there's no further argument," he said, resuming their dance. "Because the night is still young."

That was exactly what Shantel was afraid of because she had no idea what the evening held in store.

* * *

Consequences of Passion by Yahrah St. John is part of the Locketts of Tuxedo Park series.

Dear Reader,

I'm excited to start my new series, Locketts of Tuxedo Park, and introduce my sexy hero, Roman Lockett. He's an alpha and goes after what he wants: his brother's best friend, Shantel. But there's a consequence to their passion.

Shantel never wanted to be a mother, having lost hers, and she's reluctant to love again after being hurt once, but she can't deny that the sparks with Roman make her act out of character. Meanwhile, Roman is trying to live up to his father's expectations but feels like he never measures up. The couple want to do the right thing by their child, but they constantly fumble. Who can't relate to that? Add in unforgettable characters like Julian Lockett, our next leading hero, and you have the makings of a great series.

Ready for another YSJ book? Visit my website, yahrahstjohn.com, for the latest YSJ news or write me at yahrah@yahrahstjohn.com for details.

Best wishes,

Yahrah St. John

YAHRAH ST. JOHN

CONSEQUENCES OF PASSION

Recycling programs for this product may not exist in your area.

ISBN-13: 978-1-335-23284-7

Consequences of Passion

This edition published by arrangement with Harlequin Books S.A.

For questions and comments about the quality of this book, please contact us at CustomerService@Harlequin.com.

Harlequin Enterprises ULC
22 Adelaide St. West, 40th Floor
Toronto, Ontario M5H 4E3, Canada
www.Harlequin.com

Printed in U.S.A.

Yahrah St. John is the author of thirty-five books. This extroverted author has a penchant for readers who love soap operas because she grew up watching them. Yahrah writes steamy contemporary romances filled with strong, sexy heroes and feisty, independent heroines with a dash of family drama. When she's not crafting one of her spicy books, she's at home cooking a gourmet meal or traveling the globe seeking out her next adventure. Yahrah is a member of Romance Writers of America. Visit for more info: yahrahstjohn.com.

Books by Yahrah St. John

Harlequin Desire

The Stewart Heirs

At the CEO's Pleasure
His Marriage Demand
Red Carpet Redemption
The Stewart Heirs

Locketts of Tuxedo Park

Consequences of Passion

Visit her Author Profile page at Harlequin.com, or yahrahstjohn.com, for more titles.

You can also find Yahrah St. John on Facebook, along with other Harlequin Desire authors, at Facebook.com/harlequindesireauthors!

To my colleague and friend Delilah Bray
for giving me a fresh perspective by bringing
more laughter into my life.

One

Roman Lockett was bored already.

Why had he let his sister, Giana, convince him to attend this bachelor auction benefitting a cure for multiple sclerosis on a Saturday night? Because as the baby girl of the family, anytime she looked at him with those big brown eyes of hers, he was helpless to resist.

Roman's mind, however, was still on the tense meeting he'd had yesterday. As chief operating officer and director of player personnel of the Atlanta Cougars football franchise, it was Roman's job to handle all major player contract concerns. And securing DeMarius Johnson, the team's star quarterback, was high on not only his list but his father, Josiah Lockett's, the Atlanta Cougars owner and general manager.

Because of his impending fee agency, negotiations

with DeMarius had dragged on for months. His father thought Roman incapable of finishing the deal, but Roman had come to the table prepared for battle. They'd had to void the final two years of DeMarius's contract, allowing the Cougars to re-sign him while maintaining the league's salary cap. It had been risky because it was already late January. However, Roman had known allowing him to become a free agent would be problematic and so he'd adapted the contract based on market factors.

Roman hoped his father would be proud of the win under his belt. He had been on a success streak in recent years with the talent he'd brought to the Cougars team. As a result, they were ranked fifth in the league and Roman had played a big role in that. Yet despite all his successes, his father never gave him his due. Because Roman was the oldest, Josiah Lockett was harder on him than on his younger siblings, Julian, Giana and Xavier.

He stood on the outer fringes of the vast oval-shaped ballroom with crystal chandeliers and white drapery and surveyed the elegantly dressed men and women. He caught a glimpse of Giana making the rounds to get everyone psyched up for the evening. She wore a one-shouldered canary yellow gown with a stunning diamond necklace. Her jet-black hair had been artfully cut shoulder-length with bangs. It was a different look for her, but she wore it well. Meanwhile, most of the men were shamelessly flirting in the hopes women would bid outrageously on them. Roman, however, didn't need to work the room.

He was Roman Lockett and every woman in Atlanta

knew he was heir apparent to the Atlanta Cougars franchise. And if they seemed not to, they were faking it. His parents had been a major presence in the community for three decades. He'd already been approached by several beautiful women who'd made blatant attempts at seduction, and when that didn't work, they'd resorted to pouting or affected hurt, all in an effort to gain his attention. But tonight, none of them held any appeal.

Roman had no idea how he was going to make it through the rest of the night. Let alone a date with one of these insipid women. Until he saw *her*.

A caramel-skinned beauty in a blush-colored gown with spaghetti straps. It wasn't as elaborate as some of the confections he'd seen other women in tonight, showing off their God-given assets. Instead, it might be considered modest. Then she spun away and Roman saw the dress plunged to a curvy bottom, leaving her back bare save for a skinny piece of fabric holding the straps together.

For the first time tonight, Roman was intrigued. She looked oddly familiar, but he couldn't place her. *Who is she?* He had to know. He began wandering across the ballroom toward her, but was stopped by another bevy of beauties. When he finally managed to extricate himself from their clutches, Roman couldn't find her.

His nose flared. She might be the woman he wouldn't mind spending time with at the end of the evening. He prayed she would come back because only she could transform this night from being an abysmal failure.

Shantel Wilson was impressed with the image she presented. With her job as a psychiatrist she didn't often get a chance to dress up for a fancy night out on the town. Her best friend, Julian Lockett, had begged her to come and bid on him at the bachelor auction so he didn't take home some unsuspecting female.

"C'mon," Julian had cajoled. "I need your help. After that unflattering article about my dating life, my mother is furious with me. She warned me she wouldn't tolerate any more shenanigans and I agreed to keep a low profile. If you attend, she'll know I'm keeping my promise."

"I don't have anything to wear to something that fancy." Shantel had used any excuse she could to get out of the event. Her wardrobe was comprised of slacks, silk blouses and the occasional skirt.

"Don't worry about that. I know some fancy boutiques in Buckhead."

Shantel had rolled her eyes. "I'm not one of your girls, Julian. I can buy my own clothes."

"I know that, but trust me, it will help make you feel more comfortable hob knobbing with the upper crust if you're in a killer dress."

Famous last words, Shantel thought.

And so she'd gone to the high-end boutique Julian suggested and hadn't been disappointed. The sales women had been eager to help, especially when she mentioned she was attending the Lockett charity gala. They'd shown her dresses in all shapes and price tags in the hopes she'd choose the most exorbitant one. Instead, she'd opted for a simple blush dress in silk chiffon, which she could afford with her salary from the practice.

Shantel liked the way it hugged her slender curves,

and with the built-in bra, she'd been able to forgo a bra thanks to her barely B-cup-size breasts. The sales clerk insisted she needed lingerie, four-inch stilettos to boost her five-four height and a clutch to finish her look. In the end, Shantel purchased the entire ensemble. Tonight she felt like Cinderella, except she wouldn't be losing her slipper. The shoes alone cost eight hundred dollars.

She was perusing the room when her eyes caught sight of Roman Lockett. The eldest brother of the Lockett clan was tall with a commanding presence. He wore what was no doubt a custom-fit tuxedo like a suit of armor. A veneer of power clung to his athletic frame. To Shantel he was like no other man she'd ever encountered, but Roman never paid any attention to her on the few occasions she'd been in his presence.

Tonight he was clearly bored with his surroundings if the jaded expression on his face was anything to go by. Had he been coerced into attending tonight's event? And where was Julian, anyway? He'd begged her to come tonight and bid on him, but he was nowhere to be found.

Her idea of a fun Saturday night was a hot bath, a glass of wine and streaming a Netflix movie, but when Julian had pleaded with her, she'd been powerless to resist. Ever since they met at a college party ten years ago, their friendship had been grounded in love and affection. Julian had been attending Morehouse while she'd been at Spelman. Their friendship endured her mother's suicide and Julian's many love affairs, but that didn't mean he didn't vex her.

Shantel stepped out of the ballroom, pulled her phone from her clutch and texted Julian.

Where are you?

She waited and saw three dots on her iPhone indicating he was typing a message, but then the text bubble went away. She was certain Julian had read her message, so why wasn't he responding? There was no way she would have come tonight if it wasn't for him. Large social gatherings weren't really her thing. She thrived in one-on-one interactions. She supposed it was why she was so good at her job.

Having been raised on the farm and being a nerd, she'd always been socially awkward. College had been eye-opening for a simple country girl like Shantel. She'd been raised in a town where everyone knew each other, but in college she hadn't understood the rules or the games people played. Sometimes Shantel wondered if she'd made the right choice and whether she'd ever find a man who truly *got* her.

She was so deep in thought, Shantel didn't realize she had company until she looked upward and found Roman's ebony eyes trained on her.

He'd found her.

Suddenly the night he hadn't been looking forward to had taken an unexpected turn. His mood became considerably lighter as he extricated himself from several hungry females with dollar signs in their eyes to find the demure woman in the pink dress. But when he finally did, recognition dawned.

"Do we know each other?" he inquired, searching her arresting face. She wasn't classically beautiful like many of the models and actresses he typically dated, but there was a freshness to her symmetrical features, proud nose and pink kissable lips.

Her eyebrows rose and he could feel her bristle. “Is that what you say to all the ladies, Roman?”

“So you *do* know me?”

She rolled her eyes and Roman watched, transfixed, as she moved to step away from him. “Wait.” His hand jerked out to clasp around her upper arm, and a jolt of awareness rushed through him. *Does she feel it too?* It didn’t appear so because she glanced down at where he still held her, and he released her arm. “I’m sorry, but are you going to introduce yourself?”

“Roman.” She suppressed a sigh. “It’s Shantel Wilson, Julian’s friend.”

“Shantel?” He leisurely swept his gaze over her and was rewarded when a blush stole up her cheeks. “You look stunning.” He hadn’t recognized her. Her hair hung in soft curls down her back, her makeup was artfully applied and she had on killer heels making her nearly reach his chin.

“Thank you.”

“You’re welcome.” His mouth creased at the corners into a full-blown smile. “What are you doing here?”

“That brother of yours convinced me to come and bid on him and then he’s a no-show. Can you believe that?”

Roman chuckled. “I can.” Julian was known to be unreliable at the best of times.

“Anyway, I was about to leave.”

“You can’t.”

One eyebrow rose.

“I mean, if you’re already here, you might as well

stay." Roman didn't want her to leave. Shantel Wilson was the most interesting part of his evening.

"And why would I do that?"

"Because I'd like you to," he responded. "And because I need you."

A frown marred her face. "How's that?"

He leaned forward and whispered in her ear. "I need you to protect me from the women in this room." He turned her shoulder toward the ballroom. "Look at them. They're vultures and I'm fresh meat."

Shantel laughed and the sound was like an intoxicating elixir to his system. "So you'll stay?" he inquired. "You can bid on me like you were going to bid on Julian. I'll cover whatever amount it takes to ensure you're the winning bid."

"Are you sure about that?" she asked. "Some of these ladies look like they're willing to bet the farm."

"That may be so, but I'm more interested in the woman in front of me." Ever since he'd seen her walk in, he'd been unable to turn away, and it was odd given they'd met before. Usually he never gave a woman a second look, but Shantel was different.

"Well, in that case, I guess I'll stick around," Shantel said with a smirk. "I mean, I have nothing else to do."

Roman chuckled. "Don't sound so eager."

"I'm sorry," Shantel said. "I don't really know how to do this." She motioned back and forth between them.

"Do what?"

"You know." She blushed again and Roman was even more intrigued. What woman blushed at her age? Not many women surprised him, but she did. First her transformation and now a shyness he'd never noticed. Was that because she'd never fathomed a second glance?

"No, I don't know. Why don't you tell me?"

"The whole cat and mouse thing men and women do when they're dating or trying to feel each other out," Shantel responded. "I did my thesis on it back in college."

"Your thesis? What did you study?"

"Psychology," she offered. "It's important to understand people's reasoning behind how they behave."

"And did your studies provide clarity?" Roman inquired.

"Sure they did. They taught me that I don't understand a damn thing," Shantel responded with a laugh, and Roman couldn't help joining her. She had a naturalness to her missing in other women he encountered.

He wanted to learn more, but suddenly Giana was onstage announcing it was time for the Bachelor Auction to start and all participants were needed backstage. Roman hated to leave. "Will you stay?" he asked. "And bid on me, however much it takes."

"Roman…"

He liked it when she said his name and if he had his way, she'd be saying it a lot more before the night was over. "Say yes." Her eyes grew wide at the commanding tone in his voice, so he amended, "Please."

"Fine. You'd better be worth every penny."

Roman grinned widely. "Oh, I am." He left her blushing from ear to ear. It appeared the night was looking up and wouldn't be a complete bust, after all.

He made his way backstage and found Giana in a huff. He smiled into her dark brown eyes surrounded by clear chocolate skin similar to his. They'd both taken after their father's dark coloring. "There you are. We were looking everywhere for you."

"Sorry, I was otherwise engaged."

Giana smothered a laugh. "Oh, I bet you were. I've already had a half dozen women ask how much I think it'll take to win you for the night."

"Oh Lord." Roman rolled his eyes. He no more wanted to spend an evening in those women's company than he would want a root canal. It was why he was happy to have an ace in the hole. Shantel would be the winning bid and when the night was over, he had every intention of taking the delectable beauty in his arms. All night long.

Roman glanced behind the curtain and saw Shantel standing toward the back of the room. His skin tightened and his muscles surged at the sight of her. He wanted to ravish her all night long, but he could only offer her tonight because he didn't do commitment. Roman wondered what Julian would think about him getting intimate with his best friend. Would he consider it a betrayal of their brotherhood?

Just how far was he willing to go for one night with Shantel?

Two

Shantel's heart was tripping over itself. She couldn't believe the way Roman Lockett had responded to her transformation. She never imagined he'd look at her with the frank interest he'd shown tonight. In the past, he'd never paid her much attention, but there had always been something about Roman. The way he dominated the room made Shantel uneasy and she'd steered clear of him. Tonight, all dolled up, she'd felt more confident than she had in years.

Is that why he's interested?

She would have to wait and find out because Giana Lockett was back on stage and thanking everyone for coming to the Bachelor Auction. It was a worthwhile charity so Shantel didn't mind spending Roman Lockett's money.

She had no idea how competitive the bidding was going to get until it started.

An all-out war took place over several men. The first was a handsome doctor with a pair of killer blue eyes. As Giana regaled the room with a sales pitch about him, the women cheered and applauded his walk around the stage. He was swiftly followed by an up-and-coming basketball star. Two women nearly came to blows over securing him for the evening.

When it was finally Roman's turn, Shantel's hands became clammy. *What if I fail?* These women were barracudas.

"And finally, our last bachelor of the evening is none other than my big brother, Roman Lockett," Giana said. "Please give him a big round of applause."

Shantel watched as Roman walked across the stage. The man was impossibly handsome. *Impossibly.* Chocolate skin with ebony eyes and brows, a broad nose and a sexy full mouth. It was no wonder she was taken with him. Up there, he looked tall and powerful like some sort of god. With his sculpted beard, he could have been a pirate or warlord, but Roman Lockett was neither of those. He was just a man, but a sexy one.

When Roman made it to the end of the stage, his eyes searched the crowd. *Is he trying to find me?* Their eyes made contact and her mouth went dry because suddenly he was staring right at her. Shantel looked over her shoulders to make sure he wasn't looking at someone else and caught sight of the envious glares of several women. Her eyes darted upward again, and she found his gaze still locked on hers. Electricity zapped down her spine, and Shantel was thankful she was seated because she felt faint. The naked longing was evident in Roman's stare; she shifted hers downward.

"Roman Lockett is not only the best brother a woman could have, but he also has business degrees from Harvard and Wharton. He's the chief operating officer and director of player personnel of the Atlanta Cougars. When he's not overseeing the management operations for one of the largest football franchises in the US, he's a family man, spending time with the Lockett family. In his spare time, he enjoys running, racquetball, golf and traveling the world. You'll have the time of your life if you're lucky enough to spend the evening with my brother. So I'm handing him over to the charity auctioneer."

The auctioneer didn't waste any time. "We are going to start the bidding at ten thousand dollars."

It was the highest starting bid of the evening, and Shantel gasped at the exorbitant amount, but then a woman beside her raised her paddle. The auctioneer smelled blood, because he went in for more. "Can I get ten thousand five hundred?"

Another woman raised her paddle.

"Can I get eleven thousand?"

A third woman joined the bidding and held up her paddle.

Shantel glanced at Roman and his eyes pierced hers. She knew what had to be done and quickly raised her paddle. "Twelve thousand," she yelled out.

Soon it was a battle between Shantel and the three women. To her horror, the bids only went higher and higher, and Shantel paled when they hit twenty thousand dollars for one night with Roman Lockett.

"Twenty-five thousand." The woman beside Shantel smiled in her direction.

It was an outrageous sum and Shantel knew what she had to do. Go big or go home. She was certain the woman beside her had deep pockets and might be willing to go toe-to-toe.

She shot up to her feet. "Fifty thousand."

A gasp could be heard throughout the crowd. Two of the three women placed their paddles down, leaving Shantel and the other woman to fight to the death.

"You can have him," the other woman said and stormed from the ballroom.

Shantel let out a breath she didn't know she'd been holding.

"Congratulations, you'll be enjoying an evening with Roman Lockett for the special price of fifty thousand g's," the auctioneer stated. "Hope you enjoy him. Go get her, tiger!" he said when Roman hopped off the stage and marched straight toward her.

"You did it!" Roman swept Shantel into his arms. "I'm yours," he said in a rich, deep voice.

Once he returned her to her feet, he held out a hand. "Dance with me."

Shantel regarded him warily. *Is this what I signed up for?*

"I promise I don't bite," he said when she failed to comply. "Plus you'll need the fifty-thousand-dollar check I have for you."

She glanced up at him and he rewarded her with a smile. Warmth alighted in his dark gaze. Reluctantly she put her hand in his. The way his fingers curled around her palm caused a delicious heat to bloom low in her belly. It wasn't an unfamiliar feeling.

It was lust.

She saw the heat in Roman's eyes and knew he'd felt it too: that rare, intangible connection with another human being. She allowed Roman to guide her toward the dance floor even though she wanted to run. Once there, his hands went lower and slid around her waist, bringing her closer to him. So close she could smell the rich and spicy scent that was uniquely Roman. *Why have I never noticed it before?*

Because she'd never allowed herself to get close enough. But tonight she had. She didn't move a muscle when Roman's hands went to her shoulders and with a gentle brush of his fingers pushed her hair aside to whisper in her ear. "Thank you for the save."

Shantel glanced up in confusion.

"If you hadn't made such an outrageous bid, where would I be? Not with the most beautiful woman in the room."

She shook her head. "Don't say things like that, Roman. Not when you don't mean them."

She felt the warm weight of his hands on her shoulders when he stopped their dancing to say, "I mean it." His words shocked her into silence. They'd known each other for over a decade and nothing like this had ever come up.

She was out of her depth with a man like Roman. He was world-wise and moved in different circles than the academics she normally encountered. Being around him made her feel stirrings in her belly, and her blood zinged.

"Good, I'm glad there's no further argument," he said, resuming their dance. "Because the night is still young."

That's exactly what Shantel was afraid of, because she had no idea what the evening held in store.

Roman could tell Shantel was skittish. He was used to women who knew how to play the game, and he could spot an ingénue act in a second, but she wasn't one of them. If he'd known she was hiding all this beauty underneath when Julian brought her to the house, he would have made a move sooner.

Roman briefly thought about how his brother might feel about him getting involved with one of his friends, but dismissed the notion. Shantel was not one of Julian's girls. She didn't fit the profile. His profile either, if he was honest. If he was a decent guy he would let her go back to her safe world, but he didn't want to. After being jaded by Atlanta's women, she was a breath of fresh air that he didn't want to let go of.

And he wouldn't.

"So, what do you say we continue enjoying the evening without the crowd?" Roman asked. *Is she thinking I mean something more intimate?* Because she wasn't far off the mark, but Roman wasn't so uncouth as to suggest it off the bat. He would have all night to discover her secrets. "I was thinking a nice dinner someplace. I'm starved. How about you?"

"I don't know… I should probably head home."

"The night is young and I believe I owe you an evening out," Roman responded. "You did win the bid."

"With your money," she quipped.

"Humor me."

She smiled. "Fine. Dinner sounds lovely."

He linked his arm through hers and led them to the cashier. After dropping off the check, they slipped out the back doors of the ballroom and quickly made their way in the elevator to The Sun Dial at the top of the Westin. It was known for its breathtaking 360-degree views of the Atlanta skyline, and between tantalizing plates of food, they could enjoy live jazz in a soothing and sophisticated atmosphere. During the ride up, Roman didn't let go of Shantel's hand. He was afraid if he did, she'd run off like a scared colt.

The host recognized Roman when they arrived. "Jean Jacques. I know it's late," Roman began.

"We always have a table for a Lockett," the host said, grabbing two menus from the host's stand. "Please follow me."

He led them to a candlelit table for two near the window with a view of the city. Once they were seated, Shantel said, "Is this a regular occurrence? Showing up to fine dining restaurants without a reservation?"

Roman shrugged. "Name recognition. But I don't want to talk about me. I want to know more about you."

During the three-course meal, Roman discovered more about Shantel than he'd known in the last decade. She was the youngest of four children. Her father owned a farm in her hometown of McDonough, Georgia, a couple hours outside Atlanta, and her mother was deceased.

As he wiped the edges of his mouth after dessert, Roman realized he didn't want the night to end. But soon they were walking toward the front of the restaurant.

"Dinner was wonderful," Shantel said. "Thank you for such a lovely night."

Roman knew what he wanted to come next, but did she? Although her nervous blushes ended as dinner progressed, was Shantel feeling the same pull? "How about a view of Atlanta from the deck?" he asked impulsively.

"It's late. I would imagine it's closed."

"Not for us." After he spoke with the concierge, the observatory deck was opened for them. Roman called in favors only on special occasions and tonight was one of them.

After an exhilarating eighty-five-second ride in one of the glass elevators, they were taken to the View Level atop the Westin. It was a cool evening, so Roman removed his tuxedo jacket, covering her shoulders.

"Thank you." The teasing glances she gave him from underneath mascara-sooted lashes made Roman want to pull her into his arms, but she was already turning away to see the view. There were four highlighted digiboards to show Atlanta's famous landmarks. Roman stood beside her as she took in the sights, but none were as beautiful as her.

He couldn't help it. He had to have a taste.

Roman drew her backward against his body and she turned around to face him.

"You have no idea how bad I want to kiss you right now."

"Then do it," she murmured.

She didn't protest when he wrapped his arms around her and leaned his forehead against hers. Instead he felt the warm puff of her breath as it mingled with his, and his world tilted on its axis. He dipped his head until his lips met hers. It was a soft, sweet kiss, belying the raging lust he felt.

All Roman could hear was the beating of his own heart in his ears. The world was reduced to this woman in this moment in time. When she moaned, Roman deepened the kiss, parting her lips so she could taste him. His tongue slipped inside, dueling with hers. She tasted of chocolate and raspberries from the dessert they'd shared earlier. The sweetness added another layer to his already deepening desire.

"You taste so good," he murmured when they finally drew apart to take a breath.

"You do too. But why did you stop?" She was still clinging to him.

"Shantel…"

She reached up and clasped the back of his head, bringing him back to her lips. He twirled her around so that her feet left the deck, and then he was pushing her against the wall. This time he didn't hold back as he had before. He switched gears, ratcheting from soft, gentle kisses to plundering, demanding kisses until Shantel gave herself up to the passion he knew was hidden beneath the surface. He felt the tight points of her breasts against his chest and his brain short-circuited. He was burning up from the inside out. Lifting his head, he growled, "Spend the night with me, Shantel."

Three

Shantel's breath was rushed and ragged when she looked into Roman's midnight eyes. She'd never felt this kind of lust before. In high school, Shantel had been madly in love with Bobby Winfield. Her first love had been captain of the basketball team and everyone in McDonough loved him. *How could they not?* Bobby was not only good-looking at six-foot-two, but charming and gregarious. With Bobby, kisses had always been nice and sweet, but never this raging torrent of emotions. *Is this normal?*

And now, Roman was asking her to spend the night with him. How would getting physical with Roman impact her relationship with Julian? Although they'd always been friends and had never crossed the line, she doubted Julian would want her getting involved with his commitment-shy brother. She'd heard stories about Roman's escapades, which was why she was hesitant to move forward.

She'd never gone to bed with a man after one evening. She'd been deeply hurt by her breakup with Bobby. They'd made plans for their future. He would go off to college to learn how to run his family's farm and when he returned, one day they'd get married and have a slew of babies.

All her plans for her future had changed the day her father found her mother unresponsive after taking sleeping pills. By the time Shantel arrived home, it was too late, her mother was gone. Shantel had been devastated, and staying in McDonough had been impossible. Bobby hadn't wanted to leave and so they'd broken up during her freshmen year at Spelman. Instead, Shantel had become a single girl in ATL with a nonexistent sex life.

She was unprepared for the heady excitement she felt with Roman. For so long she'd denied herself the simplest pleasures in life. Perhaps tonight she should be bold. Somehow Shantel knew she was in good hands.

"Is something wrong?" Roman inquired.

"Ya think?" Shantel laughed nervously. "There's Julian."

"Are you and my brother involved?"

She shook her head.

"Have you ever been?"

"No."

"Then, let's put him aside for a moment and focus on us. What else is holding you back?"

"You."

"Me?" He seemed surprised.

"Your reputation as a ladies' man," Shantel offered. "And me, I don't—I don't do this. Spend the night with men I hardly know."

He eyed her. "But you want to, don't you, Shantel? If you do, say yes. Let's have tonight."

She looked downward, but Roman used his index finger to lift her chin, forcing her to meet his gaze. Despite her reservations that he was offering her no commitment, Shantel didn't want to miss out on an incredible night with this amazing man. Wasn't it time she lived with no regrets?

Sucking in a breath, Shantel whispered, "Yes, I'd like that very much."

Roman swept her off her feet and led her to the elevator. A wild rush of anticipation soared through Shantel when he slid her down his body to her feet. Shantel could feel the hard planes and contours of his body, and little tremors ran through her, especially when he smoothed his hands down to cup her bottom and pull her firmly to him.

Shantel gasped. It was shockingly intimate and she hadn't been with many men. Roman took full possession of her mouth and the contact of his lips on hers sent blistering heat flashing through her. She returned his ardor, opening her mouth under his and boldly mating her tongue with his. Her body ached and pulsed for him and it was exciting. She hadn't thought she was capable of feeling this sort of longing and need, but it was there, a living, breathing thing.

Shantel pushed aside any rational thoughts that this was not her typical behavior. Instead, she went with it, moaning when Roman angled his head and deepened the kiss. He knew exactly how to use his lips and tongue to mesmerize her into an erotic dance that only the two of them could share. When the ding of the elevator sounded, they parted. Roman grasped her hand and led her down the corridor in the hotel. They stopped in front of a room labeled Governor's Suite.

She looked at him questioningly.

"My family has a room we keep on standby."

Shantel wondered if this was where the Lockett men always brought their women, but she remained mum and walked inside.

She didn't pay much attention to the details of the room other than to note it was decorated in browns and beige. As she walked over to the floor-to-ceiling windows, another spectacular view of Atlanta awaited. That's when saw the king-size bed. Suddenly Roman's hands were at her shoulders, and she sucked in a deep breath when his lips pressed against the nape of her neck.

"Did I tell you," he whispered, his thumbs stroking the bare skin of her back, "how beautiful you look tonight?"

"A time or two," Shantel said, glancing into the window to look at his reflection. His hands were tracing a line down her back, his touch sparking flames. Shantel held her breath when he found the hidden zipper of her dress and edged it down.

Of course, a man like Roman would know how to get a woman out of her clothes quickly. *This* was all new to Shantel. She'd never been this daring before with other men, but then again, none of them were Roman.

Her gown loosened around her. "I love this dress," Roman said, "but it has to go."

She chuckled as it slithered to the floor. She turned to kiss him, but his eyes were devouring her bare breasts and the tiny scrap of delicate lace concealing the V at the apex of her thighs.

"God, do you have any idea what you're doing to me?" he murmured, heat flaring in his gaze. "All evening, I've been imagining what you would look like, but my dreams didn't do you justice."

He lifted his eyes to her and reached for her, cupping his large hand behind her head and slanting his mouth across hers. Their breaths mingled and tongues dueled, and once again Shantel got caught up in the fever pitch. He gave a roar of triumph and picked her up, carrying her to the bed. Shantel watched with amazement and a bit of reverence as he rose to shed his shoes and clothes piece by piece until he stood before her proud and erect.

She swallowed nervously. She was no virgin, but she didn't take going to bed with a man lightly. She'd only been with Bobby and two other men, both of whom left her feeling unsatisfied afterward. Shantel had worried it was her, that she was incapable of feeling passion, especially when her last lover advised her to read a book.

As if he sensed her anxiety, Roman leaned over and kissed her lips, his big hands threading through her hair to cup her head. Then he was lowering her backward against the pillows, and his mouth left hers so he could dip his head and draw one dark brown nipple into his hot mouth.

Her back arched as he suckled, sending pleasure straight to her core. Meanwhile, his thumb was passing back and forth over her already sensitive other nipple, teasing it into a tighter bud. She moaned and Roman moved to her other breast, opening his mouth so his tongue could circle, taste and tease the bud. Shantel melted with each mind-blowing stroke of his tongue.

"I want you so bad," he murmured when he lifted his head from his ministrations long enough to peer at her.

Shantel flushed when she felt the hard evidence of his need pressing against her body, but she wasn't afraid of it. She wanted him equally as much. "Roman..."

His hands curled into the sides of the scrap of lace at her hips and drew them down her legs. Intuitively, he knew what she needed, what she ached for. So when he slipped one finger inside her feminine folds, brushing past the tight nub of nerve endings, Shantel nearly came apart.

Oh, yes, she would give herself this. If only for one night.

Roman enjoyed seeing Shantel like this, completely undone, unraveled and at his mercy. She'd been so sweet, shying away from him before, but not now. There was no reluctance or hesitation. *Is that why I feel such a raw, fierce need to possess her?* From the moment he'd seen her tonight, he'd wanted to know how she would fit against him, and those soft curves fit perfectly. He couldn't wait to feel them beneath his body and surround himself with her.

He continued pleasuring her with his finger. She was tight, but wet. She pushed her hips against his hands, signaling she wanted more, so he added another finger, stroking in and out, while pressing his thumb against her swollen clit. A sob fell from her lips and beads of sweat began to dot her lips. He lowered his head and allowed his tongue to glide over her skin in a teasing caress. She tried to shrink away, but he didn't let her.

"Too much? Tell me what you like, Shantel, what works for you."

She shook her head and lifted herself on her elbows. "I… I don't know. I don't usually enjoy this part."

Roman frowned as he peered into her brown eyes. "Then someone was definitely doing it wrong. Let me show you how good it can be." With the palms of his hands, he pushed her back down on the bed, dropping kisses along her belly and hip bone. His fingers lightly grazed her pelvis and inner thighs, and she quivered. He parted her thighs once again and with his mouth traced the delicate folds.

Shantel shuddered at every light lick. She was wet and growing wetter by the second. Roman used all of his skill set to stroke her with his tongue until she went over the edge and shattered into pieces.

He moved upward and pressed a kiss against her temple. "How was that?"

"Incredible," she said, wonderment evident in her voice. "I had no idea it could be like that. But it's not enough."

"Tell me what you want."

"I want you to make love to me."

Roman didn't need further invitation. He reached for the protection in his pants and rolled the condom on before moving over her. She caressed his shoulders, urging him on. Resting his weight on his arms and taking care not to go too fast, he nudged her entrance. She felt so good that he surged forward, propelled by his own lust. Her body welcomed him, so he went deeper. His thrusts were slow and measured at first, but then Shantel arched her hips just right. They both groaned simultaneously, and soon their bodies found an easy rhythm all their own.

They began moving like wild things, their mouths kissing and scraping, their hands clasped together as they soared higher. It was no wonder that when quivers rippled through Shantel's body, they brought on the most powerful orgasm Roman had ever had in his life, and he erupted. A loud groan tore from his lips as Shantel stroked her hands over his back and shoulders. They continued shuddering together as pleasure burst through them. Roman fell forward on top of her.

Their bodies were damp, their breathing labored. Quickly he rolled to his side and moved away to dispose of the protection and then came back. Shantel immediately curled forward into his chest, and Roman had to admit he enjoyed being able to stroke his hands from the swell of her breasts to her waist and hip and back up again. Usually after lovemaking he was ready to shower and leave, but not with Shantel.

She was different. Special. She stirred beside him. "I guess I should go home now," she said, but there was a question in her tone.

"No, the night is still young," Roman responded. "We might as well make the most of it." He pulled her into his arms and gave her a long, passionate kiss. Soon he was inside her, filling her, making them one again.

But in the back of his mind Roman knew.

This one was trouble.

Four

Shantel woke to sunlight slipping through the gaps in the curtain. A deep sense of satisfaction coursed through her veins. She'd never before felt the pleasure she felt in Roman's arms last night. She reached out an arm, searching for the source, and came up empty. The sheets were cold.

What the…?

Shantel bolted upright. "Roman?" she called out, her eyes scanning the bedroom, but there was no one. She glanced at the chair where he'd flung off his clothes in his eagerness to be with her, but it too was empty, along with the carpet where his shoes had been.

"Roman!" She called louder this time. Swiping back the covers, Shantel padded, naked and barefoot, to the other room in the suite.

He was gone.

So this is what a one-night stand feels like? She'd heard girlfriends talk about it, and Shantel had vowed to never be like them. She'd done well, until now. At thirty years of age, it had finally happened. She'd been suckered into thinking the night might have meant more to Roman. The way he'd held her in his arms and made love to her not once, not twice, but three times last night.

Christ! She thought about how shamelessly she'd allowed him into her body and to take liberties with her she'd never allowed another man, and she'd done the same to him! But she had no one to blame but herself. She'd gotten caught up in the moment—in the allure of a magical night with a handsome man who knew exactly the right words to say.

Heading back to the bedroom, she sat on the edge of the bed and glanced at the clock. It was nearly 11:00 a.m. She would at least shower before she left and took the walk of shame in last night's dress to the garage. Thank God she hadn't used valet parking.

Propped next to the clock was a handwritten note. Shantel felt sick to her stomach, but reached for it anyway.

Shantel,
I want you to know how much I thoroughly enjoyed the evening we spent together. You're an amazing woman.
Roman

It wasn't the brush-off she'd been expecting, but his message was quite clear. Thanks for the hot sex and it was on to the next woman. Shantel was mortified. She'd rather he'd left without any note. Perhaps then their night together wouldn't feel so sordid.

She should thank Roman Lockett for the lesson, because never again would she put herself out there only to be slapped in the face.

Last night was a memory, an aberration that Shantel one day hoped to forget.

"Hello, Bachelor," Giana greeted Roman when he came for Sunday dinner at their family's ten-bedroom estate in Atlanta's Tuxedo Park later that evening. He'd spent the majority of his day trying to forget and downplay the events of the night before. And how he'd lost his mind in the arms of a caramel-eyed beauty named Shantel.

"Hey, Gigi," Roman said. He kissed her cheek. Then he glanced around the room. "Where's everybody?"

"Behind you, boy," his father, Josiah, boomed, causing Roman to turn around to see him and his mother. With his six-foot-five stature, his father towered over Roman at six feet. Josiah was an intimidating man with a wide chest and husky build, the exact opposite of him. His father had played in the league in his younger days and been sidelined by a knee injury, but he'd never given up his love for the game. Instead he'd built a successful career as an entrepreneur, which gave him the ability to buy the struggling Atlanta Cougars franchise thirty years ago.

"Hey, Dad. What's going on?" He gave his father the strong handshake he required.

"I would ask you that," Josiah replied. "Heard you made quite a splash with the ladies last night."

"All my friends were texting me about you," his mother added. "Seems like you caused quite a stir."

His mother, Angelique Lockett, was the consummate Southern woman in a floral dress with a wide skirt, cardigan and fashionable pumps. She wore her jet-black shoulder-length hair flipped as she had for years. Her smooth peanut butter complexion was marred by a frown.

"He sure did," Giana responded. "At fifty thousand dollars, Roman got the highest bid of the night."

"Wow! That's impressive," his mother said, "but then again, all my boys have a way with the ladies."

"Did someone say ladies' man?" Julian asked, walking toward their mother. He pressed a kiss to both her cheeks. "How is the most beautiful mother in the world?"

"Oh, stop." She wagged her finger at him.

Giana marched toward him with her arms folded across her chest. "And where were you last night?" she inquired. "I was supposed to have two Lockett brothers." She held up two fingers. "At least Xavier told me in advance he wouldn't make it. You were a no-show."

"I'm sorry, sis, but something came up," Julian said, his expression completely deadpan.

She rolled her eyes. "Sure it did. I could have raised a lot more money if it hadn't been for you." She pushed her index finger into Julian's forehead.

While the two of his siblings bickered about what Julian should and shouldn't have done, Roman's mind wandered back to this morning when he'd left Shantel sleeping soundly in bed. He hadn't meant to stay the entire night, but then again, they hadn't gotten much sleep because they'd been too eager discovering each other's bodies.

And what a body Shantel had. It was all soft curves, which Roman had enjoyed sinking into. He thought about how timid Shantel had been at first, but then she'd turned all fiery liquid in his arms. Throughout the night, she'd sizzled with passion and he'd lost his head, but when morning dawned, it had been clear to him what he had to do. If he allowed himself, Roman suspected Shantel was the type of woman he could get serious about, and he wasn't ready to settle down, at least not yet. Plus, there was the matter of his baby brother, who might have something to say about Roman messing around with his best friend. It was better for all concerned if he kept his distance.

They hadn't talked about seeing each other again. He was sure she understood, or at least in part, that their time together was one night only. So he'd left and purposely avoided those awkward postcoital conversations that, in the cold light of day, tended to be misunderstood. They'd both wanted each other and acted in the heat of the moment.

And now it was over. Time to move on. He'd stepped under the rain-head shower and let the water cascade over him before dressing and leaving Shantel a quick note. The problem was, all day, Roman had struggled to let go of the incredible woman he'd spent the night with.

"Everything okay, son?" his father asked. "You look a million miles away."

Roman shook his head. “Yeah, yeah, I’m fine. A little preoccupied.”

“You need to get your head back in the game. The league’s combine is first of March with the draft not far behind in April. We need to secure Curtis.”

“I’m well aware.” As director of player personnel, he handled all major contracts and the club’s salary cap as well as recruitment for the team.

“We need to be ready to trade Dustin Payne so we can get a second, maybe even a third round pick.”

“Dustin is still a good running back,” Roman responded.

“He’s aging and he doesn’t run the ball like he used to. You have to be willing to trade him and get new talent.”

This was where Roman and his father disagreed. Dustin had been a loyal player for years. He’d helped them win two championships. How could they turn their back on him because he was getting close to forty?

“You need to be more cutthroat.” Josiah grasped his shoulders and tugged him toward him. “I didn’t raise you soft, boy.”

“I’m not soft. And I’ll do what’s best for the team,” Roman said. “I know you’re the GM, but I thought you were going to let me run lead this year. Or don’t you trust me?”

“Are you men over here talking football?” his mother asked, joining them by the French doors overlooking the massive terrace and infinity pool.

“Not anymore.” His father quickly softened his tone and circled his arm around his wife’s waist.

“Good, because I want to talk about Xavier.”

"What about him?" his father said.

"Has anyone heard from him?" she inquired. "I've tried reaching out to him, but he's MIA."

"You know he gets like this around this time of year," Julian said from across the room. "He goes off to sulk."

Roman agreed. It was the off-season for football, which meant as a football commentator, their brother could vacation and relax until it was time for training camp and preseason. He wasn't involved in the combine and draft, though that didn't stop him from giving his opinion to their father and Roman on who they should consider. Perhaps they should give him more input. Maybe then he'd forget about how he'd once been the quarterback and accept his fate that he would never play football again. Xavier had injured his knee as quarterback for the team. It was so severe all the experts indicated he'd never be the same again, thus ending his career.

"That still doesn't make it right," his mother stated. "Someone needs to find him."

"I will, Mama," Roman said. As the oldest, he'd always taken the lead when it came to his siblings and nothing had changed.

His mother reached across the short distance and stroked his cheek. "Thank you, Rome." His mother used his nickname.

"Who's hungry?" his father bellowed. "Because I'm starved."

Soon the Locketts were headed into the dining room for the weekly Sunday dinner. As they sat down at the table, Roman wondered what Shantel was up to. *Is she okay? Is she upset with me for leaving her without saying goodbye?*

He doubted she'd understand just how deep she'd burrowed under his skin in one night. With Shantel a part of Julian's life, it was inevitable that one day their paths would cross again. Roman dreaded the day he'd come face-to-face with Shantel because then he would be forced to confront their attraction and feelings he'd kept buried deep.

"So, are you going to tell me how you ended up bidding on Roman Lockett at the bachelor auction?" Her friend Vanessa immediately went in for the scoop when she stopped by Shantel's cottage that evening with a bottle of merlot in tow. "Twitter is blowing up about the mystery woman who scooped the handsome bachelor up for a whopping fifty thousand dollars! I mean, where in the hell would you get that kind of money?"

"Roman gave it to me."

Vanessa's brow furrowed in confusion. "He bid on himself?"

Shantel nodded. "He didn't want any of the other women to bid on him, so he asked me to."

"Because he was interested in *you*?"

"Don't make it sound like it's beyond the realm of possibility."

"I'm sorry, Shantel. I didn't mean it that way." Her best friend peered at her strangely. "Are you okay? It's not like you to be so testy."

Shantel glanced away and busied herself with opening the wine Vanessa had brought while they sat lounging on the sofa in the living room. "I'm fine."

"Whenever you say you're fine, I know something is wrong," Vanessa replied. "Did something happen between you two?"

After uncorking the bottle, Shantel poured two generous glasses of merlot. "If you're asking if we slept together, then the answer would be yes."

Vanessa spit out the wine she'd been drinking all over her shirt. "Ohmigod!"

Shantel rushed to the kitchen for some club soda and a towel and handed it to Vanessa, who'd followed her. Vanessa began blotting the floral blouse she wore as she sat on a nearby barstool. Shantel knew she'd unceremoniously dumped this news in her best friend's lap, but Shantel had no background on how to deal with this sort of thing. Her intimate relationships with men were practically nonexistent.

After Vanessa handled the damage to her blouse as best she could, she stared at Shantel. "Okay. Tell me how it came about you ended up in bed with Roman Lockett."

Shantel sighed heavily and leaned against the bar. "I was at the bachelor auction waiting on Julian. He asked me to come, but he was a no-show. I had a beauty makeover to boost my confidence for the event. I suppose I didn't look like my normal self."

"And?" Vanessa urged her to continue.

"Enter Roman. He showed interest in me, which was flattering. Asked me to bid on him too. He agreed to cover the expense."

"Fifty thousand dollars?"

"Well, you see—there was another woman bidding who didn't appear to be standing down. I made a bold move. Roman was fine with it. He stroked the check no problem, but then he asked me to dance. And then the dance led to dinner at The Sun Dial. And dinner, well, dinner led to…" Shantel glanced at Vanessa. "You don't need me to spell it out, do you?"

"Of course not, but was it good?" Vanessa asked with a sly smile.

Shantel lowered her head. A little girl talk was one thing, but how much should she share?

"C'mon, Shantel. Don't leave me hanging."

She lifted her gaze. "It was better than good. The best I've ever had. There, are you happy?"

Vanessa stared at her, bug-eyed. "I would think you'd be in better spirits after a night with Roman. What gives?"

"Would you be if he left in the morning without a word? Correction. He left me a note, Nessa. A note, for Christ's sake! Was I so bad he couldn't face me the next morning? I would have at least thought he'd extend me that much courtesy, but then again, I know nothing about one-night stands."

Vanessa slid off the barstool she was perched on and came toward Shantel. She grabbed her hand and pulled her into a hug. "I'm sorry, girlfriend. Sometimes these things happen. Sometimes men are only there for a good time and when the party is over, they're on to the next one."

Shantel shook her head in despair as they parted. "I never dreamed *I'd* be one of those women. I've always prided myself on not putting myself in these situations. I guess I'm no better than any other woman out there. All it takes is a handsome face and I drop my panties."

"Don't be so hard on yourself. You took a chance and lived a little, which you so rarely do. It's okay to make mistakes sometimes."

"I suppose you're right. I thought..." Her voice trailed off. The night had been magical, and in the moment, Shantel thought maybe, just maybe, they could have had more than the one night, but she was wishing for the impossible.

"You two were destined for each other?"

"Something like that—" Shantel offered a weak smile "—but I was wrong."

"Now what? Please don't tell me you're going to hide behind your work again? If nothing else, this experience should have shown you you're a woman with needs that are not being met."

Shantel laughed. If Vanessa was talking about sexual needs, she was putting those on the shelf. *For the foreseeable future.*

Five

"So, what do you think, Julian?" Roman asked. "Will the injury Dustin sustained during the playoffs be healed enough for him to be back for the regular season?" Roman had come to his brother's office on Monday afternoon to talk over the condition of some of the players with injuries the past season. He needed to understand if there was a path forward to another ring or if he was deluding himself.

"I don't know, Rome," Julian said. "He's certainly doing his rehab and has the will to achieve it, but maybe Dad is right. Maybe we need to trade him."

Roman rolled his eyes. "Not you too. Can't I get some support from my little brother?"

Julian rose to his feet. "I'm giving you my professional opinion. Dustin has been playing professionally for nearly twenty years, not to mention his time in college and high school. His body has taken a lot of bumps and bruises. He's got maybe one or two good years left in him, which he can ride out with another team."

"He helped us get two championship rings."

"That was five years ago," Julian stated. "You know how Dad is. He's never going to let up on you. We had a lot of losses last year."

Roman folded his arms across his chest. "I know that." He knew what he had to do, but he didn't like it.

"Then I'm sure you'll do the right thing," Julian replied. "Speaking of that, I heard my girl Shantel saved you from a fate worse than death last weekend."

"Excuse me?" Roman had been trying not to think of the beautiful woman he'd spent the night with.

"At the bachelor auction on Saturday night?" Julian offered at Roman's blank expression. "I heard she bid fifty thousand dollars. I don't suppose you had something to do with that?"

Roman gave a half grin. "Yeah, I asked her to bid on me however much it took, same as you. What happened to you anyway?"

"I had an unexpected delay with a songstress I'd met the night before."

Roman rolled his eyes. "Yeah, I just bet you did. Shantel was a lifesaver."

"That's Shantel. She's been there for me on many occasions even when I didn't deserve it. She's loyal, you know? It's not every day you meet a woman like her."

Roman frowned. He didn't appreciate hearing his brother wax poetic about the woman who'd shared his bed, which made him curious. “So why have you never made a play for her?”

“Shantel?” Julian’s voice rose. “First off, Shantel has always been like a sister to me. It’s why I kept the Morehouse men from messing with such a good girl, because if any one of those players stepped to her and broke her heart, I would have beat them to a bloody pulp. Second, she’s the kind of woman you marry, not the kind you fool around with, if you get my drift. Third, Shantel would never put up with a player like me. She values herself too much for that. I hope she meets a man worthy of her one day, because she deserves the best.”

Yes, she did. Which made Roman feel like a jerk for having used her for one night of pleasure. But oh, what a night it was! “All right, then.” He leaned towards his brother for a one-armed hug. “Thanks for the info on Dustin. I appreciate it, and your advice won’t fall on deaf ears.”

Julian grinned. “That’s what brothers are for.”

Roman left Julian’s office as quickly as he could. It appeared that Shantel hadn’t revealed their encounter to Julian, and if she hadn’t revealed their tryst so far, Roman was going to presume she wouldn’t because Shantel didn’t strike him as the vindictive type. Roman was thankful. If his brother ever found out what went down between them, he was afraid of the rift it might cause.

“Are you ready to close up shop?” Martin Hicks, her colleague, asked Shantel when Friday afternoon rolled around.

“Almost. I’m dictating my notes for my assistant to

type up for Monday," Shantel replied. She'd been working hard with her client Alma Stevens, who'd suffered four miscarriages in the last five years. Each one had taken a piece of her client's heart and she was struggling.

"Is that the client you told me about?" Martin asked. "Is she getting any better?"

"Hard to tell," Shantel said. "I've tried to get her to bring in her spouse. They both need counseling." Therapy was a way to let go of the hurt and the pain. She only wished her mother had done the same before she took her own life.

"At the end of the day you have to remember you've done all you can," Martin replied. "You can't take it home with you."

"That's easier said than done."

"Okay, well don't work too late."

"I won't. See you Monday." Once Martin had gone, Shantel stared at the closed door. Something about Alma's desire to be a mother spoke to Shantel. It wasn't as though she was eager to become one herself. Quite frankly, it was the opposite. If her own mother was a manic depressive, what would happen to her child? Although Shantel had no mental health issues, it didn't mean her offspring wouldn't. Sometimes bad genes skipped a generation.

Yet Alma's desperation to give her husband a child was so raw. It was sometimes hard for Shantel to regroup after their sessions. That was why she'd changed Alma's appointment to be her last for the day. There was no way she could switch on and off between clients when one of them took so much out of her emotionally.

The week had dragged on and on for Shantel. And she knew why. Some deep-down part of her had hoped Roman would see the error of his ways and call or text her, but that day never came. And so with each passing day, her ire went up. She needed an escape, which was why she'd agreed to attend an art gallery opening with Julian. The younger Lockett was always a lot of fun and would help pull her out of her funk. Julian's personality was so far removed from his older brother's, Shantel could easily put his relationship with Roman to the side.

After going home for a quick shower and change of clothes, she was ready at 7:00 p.m. when Julian rang the doorbell.

"Well, damn!" he said when she swung open the door.

Confidence boost. Check.

Shantel had chosen to wear a midi dress with a black ruched see-through overlay. It was a trick of the eye because you might think she was naked, but she wasn't because there was a nude dress underneath. She couldn't wear much lingerie because it would show panty lines; she'd opted for a thong and no bra.

"You look hot!" Julian said, kissing her on the cheek. "I'm going to have to beat the men off with a stick tonight."

"Oh, stop!" She couldn't help enjoying the attention. "Anyway, thanks for the invite. I'm sure you have better things to do than spend your time with me."

Julian snorted. "It's no chore, Shantel. You know I love ya and I'm free tonight, so you're in luck. C'mon."

After locking up her cottage, Shantel eased herself into Julian's Bugatti Veyron. The man loved fast cars and *fast women.* On the drive, they caught each other up about their weeks, and soon they were pulling up outside the gallery.

"The artist is a friend of mine from Morehouse," Julian said, handing the valet his car keys and leading her inside. "He dropped out because college wasn't for him, but I always knew he would be great someday, so I'm here to support him."

Shantel touched Julian's arm. "You're a good friend." Suddenly the hairs on the back of her neck stood at attention. She spun on her strappy sandaled heel but didn't see anything out of the ordinary in the foyer. *So why does it feel as if I am being watched?*

"C'mon." Julian linked arms with Shantel. "I'll introduce you to my friends."

Shantel glanced around one more time but merely saw several people milling about, looking at the art on display. She was being overly dramatic. It wasn't like she knew anyone else here.

Why?

That's the question Roman asked himself as he stood beside Keke Wyatt, the hot new model on Instagram. They'd met at a football industry party some months ago, and she'd indicated she was in town for the weekend. He'd been desperate to escape the endless movie reel loop he'd felt like he'd been on the last week. He hadn't been able to escape seeing Shantel come apart in his arms. He could still hear her soft moans and pants when he'd been buried deep inside her. He remembered the way her legs clutched his hips as she'd taken him someplace no woman ever had.

Nirvana.

So when Keke suggested a low-key night out at an art gallery opening she'd heard about from some friends, he'd agreed. They would have a few drinks and see where the evening led.

He hadn't expected Julian to bring Shantel to the opening. They didn't travel in the same social circles. Roman could count on one hand the number of times he'd run into her over the last decade she'd been friends with his brother.

And now?

Two weekends in a row? *What are the odds I'd run into my one-night stand a week after unceremoniously leaving her a note on the nightstand?* It was beyond inconceivable.

So here he was with Keke, hiding out on the other side of the gallery, staring at Shantel like some hopeless dope. She looked like a million bucks in some sheer number that showed off her killer legs and clung to all her curves. Curves he'd gotten to know very well the weekend prior.

Damn.

He couldn't think of a way out without her seeing him. He would have to bluff his way through it.

"What do you think of this one?" Keke pointed to an abstract piece of art that for the life of him Roman couldn't figure out. With a myriad of colors from black to pink to gold to turquoise, it looked like a wave, but he could make out a face, as well. "It's interesting, right?"

"Yeah." Roman circled his arm around her waist and turned her so they weren't facing Shantel. "What do you say we get out of here?"

"Roman?" Julian bellowed to him from across the

room. He couldn't very well ignore his brother, so Roman spun around and came face-to-face with Julian and Shantel.

Shantel glanced at him and then at Keke and then back to him. A hurt look crossed her beautiful face, but then, just as quickly, she was stone-faced, and he couldn't tell what she was thinking. The night they'd spent together, he'd been able to tell exactly what she was feeling, but she gave nothing away tonight.

Julian walked toward them. "Hey, Rome. What are you doing here? Didn't think you were an art connoisseur."

"He's not," Keke said. "I suggested it."

"Julian. This is Keke Wyatt. Keke, this is my brother, Julian Lockett," Roman said, making the introductions.

Julian grinned as he sidled next to Keke. "I knew it. Rome wouldn't know a Van Gogh from a Picasso."

Roman glared at his younger brother, who for some reason couldn't take his eyes off *his* date while Roman couldn't stop staring at Shantel. "Thanks a lot, Julian."

"Oh, no problem," Julian said distractedly. "How would you feel about me showing you some of my friend's work upstairs?" he asked Keke directly. "He has some great pieces."

"You don't mind, do you, Roman?" She batted her eyelashes at him. Roman didn't care because he'd be left alone with Shantel. She was upset and wouldn't even look at him. She was staring beyond his shoulder as if he didn't exist.

"No, of course not," Roman said and watched as Keke and Julian climbed up the stairs. He turned to Shantel, but she was making a beeline for the exit.

"Wait! Shantel, wait!" Roman's voiced pitched up an octave, which caused her to halt her steps, but she didn't turn around.

"Let me go, Roman," Shantel said, her back to him.

"I can't do that. Not until we talk."

She spun around so quickly, Roman wasn't prepared for the glower on her face. "The time for that was *after* we slept together," she hissed in a whisper only he could hear. "If you'll excuse me." She reached for the door handle, but Roman grabbed her arm.

"Please don't leave like this."

"Don't touch me!" Tension emanated from Shantel and he noted her face was pinched.

He deserved that and then some. "I'm sorry, Shantel. Is that what you want to hear?"

She shook her head, frustration etched across her beautiful caramel features. Her pink-tinted lips pursed into a frown. "The only reason you're sorry is that you've been forced to face me when you'd rather sneak out like some thief in the night. But I can take a hint. So why don't you take this one—I don't wish to see you again."

Roman didn't believe that for a second. If she didn't care, she wouldn't be so upset. He clasped her arm and walked with her to a nearby alcove where there were no patrons.

"You have no right to manhandle me." Shantel's eyes were blazing fury.

And damn it, it turned Roman on. He'd seen the shy, sweet side of Shantel, but he hadn't yet encountered this fiery persona. He liked both with equal measure. *Is something wrong with me? Why does this woman affect me like no other?* He'd tried to convince himself he'd imagined the chemistry that had simmered between them that night. All week he'd been tied up in knots, punishing himself by working late or with grueling workouts at the gym in an attempt to relieve his frustration, but his body knew better. His body knew there was only one way to assuage the carnal hunger she'd ignited within him.

Often over the last week, he'd fantasized about kissing her again because her mouth promised heaven. On the other hand, he'd worried about Julian and how he might react. But his brother could care less about absconding with Roman's date! And then, of course, there were the feelings Shantel evoked in him, feelings he'd tried to avoid. But it was useless; his body ached for her. And now if he didn't kiss her again he would die.

"Shantel, I'm sorry if I manhandled you. That wasn't my intent. Tell me you want this as much as I do," he growled.

She nodded, so Roman covered her lips with his, sending his world up in flames.

Why had Shantel not sensed the change in Roman sooner? She only became aware of the thick sexual tension when her own heart began thudding hard and fast in her chest. She was furious he could just turn it on and off. One week he was with her and the next with a sexy model. Shantel was livid, but that didn't stop desire from shooting through her veins at the touch of his lips.

Her nipples turned into turgid peaks and her thong was wet with molten heat. She was aware of Roman's muscled strength as he wrapped his arm around her and decimated any vestiges of control she thought she had erected against him. Instead he laid claim to her mouth and gave a low growl when her lips parted of their own volition to allow his tongue access to her. He kissed her with utter abandon as if they weren't in an art gallery where anyone could see them making out. And she let him.

When he eased back to look at her, there was a fierce glimmer in his eyes. "Come home with me so I can make love to you properly."

His words were like being doused in cold water.

She'd done it again! Gotten caught in the haze of sexual excitement. It was as if she was spellbound by the myriad of sensations Roman induced with his kisses. *What must he think of me?* She was disgusted with her undignified behavior and pushed at his chest hard until he let her go.

She was a fool.

She would never mean anything to Roman other than an easy lay. But she'd never been that for any man before and he was no exception. "I'm not going anywhere except home."

"I don't understand," Roman said in a clipped tone. "We both want each other and we're consenting adults. Why deny yourself when it's clear your body wants me?"

Shantel looked down and could see the outline of her puckered nipples through the sheer dress she wore. She wanted to die from embarrassment, but instead she used anger to hide her vulnerability. "That line might work for you with your other women, Roman Lockett, but not with me. I won't have another one-night stand with you or an affair or whatever else it is you're looking for. Not now. Not ever. Go find your date."

Without another word, she turned on her heel and walked out of the art gallery.

Six

"I really believe your son will like it in Atlanta, Tim," Roman told Curtis Jackson's father, who'd accompanied him for a drink on Friday afternoon during the league's combine in Indianapolis. Roman was trying to get him over to his way of thinking. He'd even dressed casually in khaki pants, a polo shirt and a sports coat. He knew Tim thought him something of a stuffed shirt and he wanted to appear friendly and approachable. "Atlanta is a great city and has a lot to offer in terms of culture and black history."

"I understand all that," Tim said. "But Curtis would be far from home and I've seen and heard the stories of young men who get caught up in the game, Lockett. I want my son to stay grounded, which is why I can't guarantee you he'll sign with the Cougars."

"Surely you see the advantages in going with a black-owned team, Mr. Jackson. We pride ourselves on treating our players like family and they're paid handsomely. In addition, they are cared for by my brother Julian, one of the top sports doctors in the business, and marketed by my sister, Giana, who'll help ensure they get the best endorsement deals. We are a one-stop shop."

"You talk a good game, Lockett, I'll give you that."

"Call me Rome," he said with a smile. "All my friends do."

Tim nodded. "It's going to take a lot more than smooth talking to convince me, Rome. Actions speak louder than words."

"Then please, allow me to invite you down to Atlanta before the draft in April. See our fair city. Come meet my family, so you'll know your son is in good hands. I promise you, you won't be disappointed."

Tim pointed at him. "All right, Rome. I'll take you up on it."

"Excellent." Roman gripped his hand for a shake. "My assistant will contact you soon and make the arrangements."

He watched the older man walk off and once he was gone, threw back the whiskey he'd been nursing. After discovering the older man didn't drink, Roman certainly wasn't going to overdo it in his presence. Tim already had nerves about him and he didn't want to give Curtis another reason to consider a different team.

"How did it go?" Giana asked, sliding onto the barstool Tim had vacated. She and Julian had accompanied him to the combine, but his brother was nowhere to be found. Gigi looked sophisticated in a red power suit with ankle pants and a lace cami, her hair pulled back into a sleek ponytail.

Roman glanced at her. "How do you think?"

"You always knew he was going to be a hard sell," Giana replied. "You just have to convince him we're the best game in town."

"Like you're going to convince Wynn Starks to pay for billboards advertising his sports drink at the stadium?" Roman inquired. He knew his sister had been trying to get a meeting with the elusive billionaire bachelor for weeks and had been as unsuccessful as he'd been with winning over Tim.

Her dark brown eyes narrowed on him. "You sound like you don't think I'm up to the task, but then again, why should I be surprised? You and Daddy always do this."

"Do what?"

"Underestimate me," Giana said, rising from the barstool, "but don't you worry. I'll prove you wrong and land Wynn Starks." She sashayed away as swiftly as she'd come, leaving Roman to chuckle at his feisty sister.

She reminded him of another spirited lady he'd been unable to forget. Shantel had dressed him down the night he'd run into her at the gallery a month ago and her words had stayed with him. He couldn't blame her for her reaction. He'd been a jerk, thinking they could pick up where they'd left off as if nothing had happened. He'd slept with her and crept out, as she'd said, like a thief in the night, leaving a note behind. It was no wonder she wasn't interested in giving him a second chance.

And he'd respected her wishes.

He'd thought of her often, though, wondered if he should call or text her, but he was certain she wouldn't respond and Roman didn't do failure. Not of any kind, which was why he had to figure out how to get Curtis to sign with the Atlanta Cougars.

Otherwise, his father would never step down as general manager of the organization and *he* would forever live in his shadow.

"I think he blames me, Dr. Wilson," Shantel's client stated as she sat in her office that afternoon. Alma Stevens looked terrible. Her blond hair hung limply to her shoulders and didn't appear as if she'd washed it in days. Her usually well-dressed client wore sweatpants, a T-shirt and a hoodie.

Shantel wished she was wearing such comfortable attire. The last few days she'd felt tired and lethargic. This morning she'd barely made it out of bed even though she'd gone to sleep early. Her stomach had been upset and she was not feeling her best, but she'd come to work because she didn't want to let Alma down. She felt like the woman was on the edge of a possible breakdown.

"We've talked about this, Alma. You mustn't think this way."

"How can I not, when Brian and I both know I'm the reason our babies can't make it?" Alma cried. "It's my womb," she clutched her stomach, "that's incapable of carrying them to term. This last one, I went on bed rest after the procedure, hoping to have a better outcome, but after three months..." Fat tears slid down her plump cheeks. "It hurts so much, Dr. Wilson."

"Have you considered other options?" Shantel asked

gently. She'd been hoping to broach the subject to Alma's husband, Brian, but he'd refused to join in the therapy. Maybe he was too proud to admit *he*, *they* needed help.

"You mean surrogacy?" Alma's voice rose slightly. "Or adoption?"

"Both are viable options."

"I don't want anyone else to carry my baby!" Alma cried. "I want to!"

"It's all right, Alma. Please calm down. I didn't mean to upset you."

"You didn't. I feel like a failure and inadequate as a wife. I can't give my husband the one thing he wants more than anything."

"More than you?" Shantel leaned over to her side table to pull out several tissues and hand them to Alma. She couldn't imagine that to be true, but Alma shrugged.

"Maybe." Alma blew her nose. When she finally glanced up, her eyes were rimmed with red. "The other night I told him I'd leave him so he could find a woman capable of having children. He didn't say anything, Dr. Wilson. He sat there stone-faced. It broke my heart." She cried into her Kleenex. "I wished he would say he wanted me no matter what." She shook her head. "But he didn't."

Shantel got up from her seat and went over to hug the young woman. She knew she was supposed to maintain some professional distance, but she couldn't bear to see the woman in pain and *not* comfort her. "It's okay, Alma." She rubbed Alma's back as the woman shook with grief. "It's going to be okay."

As their session was ending, nausea struck Shantel. She barely made it to the restroom. Luckily it was gone quickly and she was able to resume her schedule.

Her partner, Martin, knocked on her door and poked his head in. "Everything okay?" he inquired. "I couldn't help but notice you seem a bit out of sorts."

"It's nothing," Shantel replied. "Just something I ate at lunch."

"If you think that's all it is..."

"What else could it be?" Shantel replied. She would get some rest tonight and then head to McDonough for her nephew Christopher's baptism tomorrow. With her family's love and a whole lot of good cooking, she would be as right as rain.

"It's great to finally have you home for a visit, baby girl," George Wilson said when Shantel came home to McDonough the following afternoon. The baptism was tomorrow and she'd wanted to come a day early to spend time with her father and siblings.

Unfortunately, she hadn't driven over from Atlanta as early as she would have liked. When she'd woken up, she'd struggled with nausea and thrown up last night's pizza. After a hot shower and sips of ginger ale and crackers, she'd finally been able to hit the road. There was no way she was missing seeing her baby nephew.

"I told you I'd be home soon." Shantel accepted her father's warm embrace as he led her inside the house.

"Yeah, well, I wasn't sure," he responded. "Come on in. Have you lost some weight?"

Shantel glanced down at the simple floral sundress she'd chosen to wear. Usually it clung to her curves, but now it hung off her. She supposed she had lost a few pounds the last week or so with the stomach bug. "Maybe a little."

"C'mon, I'll fatten you right up. Mrs. Mabel made your favorite pound cake with fresh strawberries." He walked her to the kitchen, dropping her luggage in the hallway as he went. It sounded good, but Shantel's stomach churned.

"Mrs. Mabel?" Shantel inquired, sitting down at the kitchen table as her stomach rebelled. She knew her father had been spending time with the widow, but was there more to their relationship?

"Yes, darling," her father replied, sitting across from her. "She and I have gotten closer."

"Oh, I didn't realize things had gotten that serious," Shantel replied, but should she be surprised? It had been nearly a decade since her mother had taken her own life. She couldn't expect her father, who was still in his prime, to be alone. She wouldn't want that for him because she knew was it was like.

Over the last month, she'd thought about Roman Lockett often and what might have been. The night of the art gallery opening, he'd been willing to sleep with her, but then what? After he'd tired of her, he would cast her aside for the next woman who came along. Shantel refused to be used no matter how much her body might ache for the satisfaction Roman could provide.

"Shantel?" Her father broke through her thoughts. "Where did you go just now?"

She shrugged. "I'm sorry, Daddy. I'm happy for you, and if spending time with Mrs. Mabel is what you want, then go for it."

He reached across the short distance between them and cupped her cheek. "Thank you. I was worried that after your mama, you might not accept another woman in my life."

She patted his hand. "Mama's been gone for years, Daddy. There's no reason for you to stay in this big house by yourself, paying homage to ghosts of years past. Live your life."

"I would say the same to you," her father responded.

Shantel frowned. "What do you mean?"

"Who was the last man you've dated, Shantel? I mean seriously dated."

"You know who. Bobby."

"Shantel, that's nearly a decade ago. You need to take your own advice and move on with your life. You're young. You can have a full, rich life with a husband and whole slew of babies."

She shook her head and rigidly held her tears in check. "Daddy, I'm just not sure I'm mother material."

"Why not? Because of your mama's mental health issues?"

She nodded. She wasn't sure she could ever bring a child into the world after what had happened with her mother's mental illness. Shantel didn't want to risk passing that down to her children.

"Why would you think the worst?"

Shantel shrugged, feeling distracted. All this talk of babies made a thought flit through her brain.

When was my last period?

The front door sprung open and in poured Shantel's brothers Terrance, Frank and Bernard, and their wives, Lisa, Charlene and Monique. They had five nephews and nieces between them. The newest addition to the family was Frank's son, Christopher, who was born a mere two weeks ago.

Immediately, Shantel reached for her nephew. He was the cutest thing, with chubby cheeks, dark brown eyes, soft chocolate skin and a head full of hair.

"It's so good to see you, Shantel," Charlene said. "But are you sure you're okay? You look a little green around the gills. Was the drive to McDonough too much?"

Shantel swallowed the bile rising in her throat and nodded.

"Why don't we get you settled for a laydown?" Charlene fussed over Shantel like she was one of her children, but at the moment Shantel didn't care. She could use a little looking after from her family. She shouldn't have stayed away so long.

When they made it to the guest room, Charlene pulled back the quilt on the bed and motioned her forward, but Shantel couldn't hold back and rushed into the bathroom, slamming the door behind her.

Afterward, she dampened a washcloth and pressed it to her forehead. When she glanced in the mirror, Shantel was horrified by how bad she looked. She was going to have to slap on makeup before her family figured out something was wrong with her.

She came out of the bathroom and found Charlene sitting in the chair next to the bed. "How far along are you?"

"Excuse me?"

"You're pregnant, right?" Charlene asked, holding the covers so Shantel could slip underneath the quilt. "I mean, I was like that with my first. They call it morning sickness, but it was all day sickness for me, but after the first few months it went away. I kept a steady stock of crackers in my purse."

"I'm not pregnant," Shantel said as she crawled into bed.

Charlene gave her an incredulous look. "Forgive me, Shantel, but if there's one thing I know after bearing three children, it's pregnancy. When was your last period?"

"Please, Charlene. I don't want to do this." Shantel shook her head.

"Shantel." Charlene sat down beside her on the bed and chastised her. "You also can't put your head in the sand. If you're pregnant, you have to start eating right, taking prenatal vitamins and go for your first checkup."

"You don't understand, Charlene. I can't be pregnant. I was only with the man one time. One night."

"I'm afraid that's all it takes."

Wasn't there some small part of Shantel that had known pregnancy was the explanation for her nausea, loss of appetite and sensitive breasts? But she'd ignored the signs because she hadn't wanted to accept that five weeks ago, she'd had sex with Roman Lockett. They'd used condoms each and every time though they were known sometimes to fail. How was it possible she'd screwed up so royally?

Tears streamed down her cheeks and she began to sob. Charlene didn't judge her; she held Shantel in her arms until she cried it out.

When it was over, Charlene handed her some Kleenex to wipe her face. "You're going to have to get a test and find out for sure, but if you need anything I'm here for you."

"Thank you."

But Shantel didn't need a test to tell her what she already knew. She was pregnant with Roman's baby.

The next morning, Charlene came to the house under the guise that she wanted to talk with Shantel about a friend in need of counseling, but that was far from the case. She'd gone to the grocery store and obtained pregnancy tests.

"I brought a few," Charlene said, holding up the brown paper bag after they'd retreated to Shantel's bedroom and closed the door. "In case of any false positives."

Shantel accepted the package. "Thank you." She grabbed one of the boxes out of the bag and read the instructions. Then she glanced at the bathroom door. Once she went in, there was no turning back. She wouldn't be able to hide from the truth.

"Go." Charlene urged Shantel on. She did as ordered, taking the entire bag with her into the bathroom. She chose one of the tests and reluctantly peed on the stick.

Then she waited.

Hoped.

Prayed for a different outcome.

But in the end all four tests were positive.

She was indeed pregnant.

Charlene knocked on the door. "What's happening? What do they say?"

After washing her hands, Shantel opened the door and held up one of the sticks. "They say I'm pregnant."

Seven

Shantel stared through the window of her office on Monday as the world passed by. It seemed the same, but had changed dramatically. She hadn't been prepared to see the two lines on the pregnancy stick this weekend. She'd steadfastly told herself that her illness could be attributed to a bug or something she'd eaten.

But a baby?

She had never wanted a child of her own, but now that it was here, she had to face the truth. And her own fears that someday, a child of hers might become unwell like her mother. She'd heard it all her life. Whispers in the small town about her "crazy" mother. Shantel and her brothers had been mocked, but her brothers hadn't cared. They'd told her to ignore the bullies. *It's just words*, they'd said, but Shantel had always taken it to heart. She hadn't been able to shrug it off, not when she'd needed someone to talk to, to confide in about becoming a woman. But her mother had been incapable of being there for her. Shantel had to muddle through puberty mostly on her own, with a little help from the school nurse.

It had been terrifying, but she'd pulled through. She'd become a psychiatrist to help people like her mother with their problems, all the while worrying that she might turn out like her mother herself. She'd graduated with a master's degree in psychology with a concentration in mental health. Then she'd gone to medical school and done a four-year residency. It had been a long road, but a rewarding one.

She'd taken pride in being responsible. And now, she'd gone and gotten herself knocked up by one of the biggest players in Atlanta. Roman Lockett had only wanted her because she was an anomaly, different from the women he usually encountered. He hadn't wanted to get to know her, except in the biblical sense. As much as she'd wanted to be with him, Shantel had known it was a mistake. But they'd created something precious.

Shantel glanced upward, praying for a sign of what to do, when a knock sounded on her door. She rose to open it and found Julian on the other side.

"Are you busy?" he asked.

"No, I don't have any clients right now."

"Good." He swept past her into the office, leaving Shantel to close the door. "Why haven't you been returning my calls? I had a big fight with my father and I needed to talk to you," he said. "Did I do something to upset you?"

Shantel shook her head. “Of course not. I’ve been really busy.” She walked past him to her desk and began searching files, eager for a distraction.

“You’ve never been too busy for me,” Julian countered as he walked toward her and leaned against her desk. And he was right. She always made time to lend an ear if he needed it. But lately, her plate had been too full with her own problems to be a sounding board for Julian.

“Things change,” Shantel said, sweeping her sweater duster around her shoulders. It wasn’t as if Julian could see she was pregnant. It was way too soon, but now that he was here, Shantel felt guilty knowing she hadn’t yet shared her condition with his brother. And Shantel wasn’t sure when she would be ready.

Julian touched her arm and turned her to face him. “What’s wrong?”

“Nothing.”

“Bull. There are dark circles around your eyes and you look as if you haven’t seen a good meal in days. Have you lost weight?”

“Really, Julian. Why do you care? I’m sure you didn’t come here to inquire about my health. What new woman has you tied up in knots?”

Julian stared at her as if she’d sprouted horns. “Damn, Shantel. I’m sorry to have burdened you with my troubles. I’ll look for another shoulder to cry on.”

As he turned to leave, Shantel called after him. “Wait! I’m sorry, Julian. I’m a bit testy these days. Please forgive me.”

Julian perked up and a broad smile replaced the frown marring his handsome face. “It’s all right. We all have a bad day, and it looks like you've seen a few lately. How about I take you out for lunch? We can have a big juicy burger with pickles, sautéed onions and mushrooms."

The thought of red meat made Shantel's stomach roil. She bolted out of her seat and rushed to the en suite bathroom in her office. She barely made it in time before she emptied the contents of her stomach in the toilet. She was going to have to see a doctor soon, but she hadn't wanted to have her worst fear confirmed.

Julian was banging on the door. "Shantel, are you okay?"

After flushing the toilet and rinsing with mouthwash, Shantel wiped her mouth and opened the door to the bathroom. She must have jumped up too quickly from the toilet because suddenly she felt as if the earth was swallowing her up. Those were her last thoughts as she fainted in Julian's arms.

"You've made very little progress moving the needle with Curtis," Josiah Lockett told Roman later that day.

"That's not true. He's agreed to come to Atlanta to see our facility and meet with us in person. I wanted him to be assured his son would be in good hands."

"Yeah, well, I would have inked the deal already," Josiah stated. "You clearly aren't offering him the right package. Perhaps he needs more incentive with branding and marketing. Giana can help you with that."

"Yes, she can," Roman said, "and she has. We've already laid out a brand strategy we think works for his clean-cut image, but he's still hesitant to sign with us. I think he has his heart set on a team in the North."

Josiah rolled his eyes. “But other teams don’t have the best state-of-the-art facility in the country. We do. Who else has an elevated pitch next to the coaching offices, so plays can be run on the fly without going back down to the fields?”

“No need to preach to the choir, Dad,” Roman replied. “I know all this.”

“And yet you can’t manage to get the job done. Maybe I’ve been backing the wrong horse all these years.”

“What the hell is that supposed to mean?” Roman asked. He hadn’t gone to Harvard and Wharton business school for no reason. Roman was sick and tired of his father putting him down after all the hard work, sweat and tears he’d put into the family business.

“I mean,” his father boomed, “Giana is begging and pleading to do more. Perhaps I should have been showing her the ropes instead of paying for that expensive education of yours if it’s not going to yield dividends.”

“I’ve had enough of your tirade, Dad. I’m tired,” Roman said and headed toward the door.

“At your age, I had already bought and sold several companies and married your mother. I mean, you’re near thirty-five years old and you’ve yet to give me a single grandchild.”

Roman spun on his heels. “And why would I want to do that, Dad? Why would I want to bring a child into this family? So you can make them feel less than like you’ve done me?”

“I have given you everything, Roman.”

But your love, he wanted to say, but uttering the words would only make him appear weak to Josiah, and Roman didn't want the fallout. It was better that he leave now.

"Roman, wait," his father started, but he was already out the door. As always, they were at odds and it was getting old. Josiah's lack of trust and faith made Roman start considering his options. He'd been approached by another franchise in need of a general manager as well as a Fortune 500 firm looking for a CEO. With his MBA and prior management skills, the Atlanta Cougars wasn't the only show in town, but it was the job he'd trained for his entire life. Who was better qualified than him to run the family business?

Shantel was silent on the drive back to her cottage. After she'd fainted at her office, Julian had taken her to the emergency room where, after several blood tests, the doctor had come to the room and congratulated Julian.

Julian hadn't understood at first, but then realization dawned when the doctor began talking to Shantel about his recommendation for an ob-gyn and suggested prenatal vitamins along with prescribing some anti-nausea medication that wouldn't hurt the baby.

The baby.

Her pregnancy was no longer a figment of her imagination or two lines on a pregnancy test. There was no more putting her head in the sand. The doctor had confirmed she was five weeks along, perfectly lining up with the night of the bachelor auction. Not that there was any doubt of who the father was, but had Julian put two and two together?

She'd never seen him rendered speechless, but he hadn't spoken to her after the doctor's proclamation. Instead, he'd stared at her long and hard and then walked out of the room.

He hadn't returned until she was being checked out, and even then, he hadn't said much. He'd bundled her into the passenger seat of his Bugatti and given her a ride home.

When they made it to her cottage, Shantel noticed her car in the driveway. Julian must have arranged to have it brought to her when he'd taken her purse at the hospital. Although she appreciated his kindness, she couldn't bear the silent treatment any longer. "Aren't you going to say something?"

He turned to glare at her and Shantel sucked in a deep breath. *He knows.*

"Exactly when did you plan on telling me I was going to be an uncle?"

Okay, so he had put two and two together.

"Before you answer me, you'd better think long and hard about whether you want to ruin a twelve-year friendship," Julian said once he'd walked her inside and closed the door.

Shantel swallowed the lump in her throat. "I..." But no words came out. She sat still for several moments, collecting her thoughts, and then tried again. Her brows furrowed and she asked, "How did you know?"

"That you slept with my brother?" Julian asked, frowning. "It was a hunch, but I wasn't certain until you confirmed it just now."

"I never said anything, and Roman doesn't strike me as the sort to kiss and tell, so why would you even go there?"

"Roman asked about you after the bachelor auction.

It struck me as odd because you're not really Roman's type, but he's been out of sorts lately. Unsettled with his life. That night, you would have been something of a novelty. I can see how he would have been drawn toward you as I was the first time we met. Except our relationship has always been a platonic one, but that doesn't mean I haven't always known you were a special person, Shantel. Your capacity to be so kind, caring and compassionate. I suppose it's why I never crossed the line with you, because I never wanted to lose you."

Tears slid down Shantel's cheeks at Julian's words. It was the most vulnerable she'd ever seen him. "And I've disappointed you?"

He shook his head. "No, not at all. You were innocent in this. But not Roman. He knew better. He knew you weren't one of his one-night stands. Yet he used you for his own pleasure."

"It's not his fault, Julian," Shantel replied. "He wasn't the only one in the room when we…"

"Created a life?" Julian offered.

Shantel nodded. "I know I should tell him."

"He has a right to know." There was no denying the demanding tone in Julian's voice.

"I was trying to figure it out and make my peace with the situation first. It's been rather shocking. A baby was never in my future." She'd thought about not having the baby or even putting it up for adoption. But at the end of the day, Shantel discovered that although she may not have planned the pregnancy, she wanted to keep her baby.

"You shouldn't have to go through this alone," Julian responded. "Roman should be here because he's equally responsible for where you find yourself now, and I'm going to see he makes things right." He started for the door, but Shantel tugged on his arm.

"Julian, no!" But he was stronger than her and gently removed her hands and left. Shantel knew there was no stopping him. Julian had decided he was going to give Roman a piece of his mind.

Why does he have to go all macho on me and confront his brother like some avenging warrior? She was no fair maiden and she could stick up for herself.

Mind made up, she grabbed her purse and rushed out the door. She had to talk to Roman before Julian did.

Eight

With a tumbler of whiskey in hand, Roman paced the floor of his home. He'd lived in the guesthouse on the Lockett estate ever since graduating Wharton. Why had he let his father get to him earlier? Hadn't he learned he was never going to please the man? Even if he hadn't already signed DeMarius or considered trading Dustin, his father would have raised the bar yet again.

It was time he faced facts. His father wasn't going to step down as general manager anytime soon and Roman jumping through hoops wasn't going to change the status quo. Josiah Lockett liked being in charge and handing down the almighty edicts. He would never give up control any more than Roman would. He supposed it was why they butted heads—because they were so much alike—but that didn't mean he would continue to be his father's whipping boy either.

In the last fifteen years, he'd proven he had the business acumen to run the Atlanta Cougars franchise, and if his father didn't recognize it, he had to consider other alternatives. If he chose to run another football franchise as general manager, he would have autonomy over most decisions other than having to run contractual issues by the owner for final approval. It wasn't his first choice to leave because the Cougars franchise was rightfully his. He'd thought it was his destiny, but maybe he was wrong?

He was thinking about his next move when he heard the crunching of gravel in the driveway outside. Pulling the drapes back, Roman saw Julian emerge from his Bugatti. He wondered what was going on because his brother walked with a purpose. He didn't have long to find out because Julian burst through the front door.

"Julian, what the hell?" Roman began, but before he could get another word out, his brother charged at him, knocking the tumbler out of his hand and sending shards of glass in every direction.

Roman glanced at the mess, but didn't have time to react because his brother punched him in the jaw. He recoiled backward, stumbling into the couch. "What was that for?" Roman asked, holding his throbbing jaw. When he looked up at Julian, his face was etched with rage and he looked like he was going to take another swing at him.

"Oh, don't play dumb now," Julian said, punching a fist into his hand. "You know exactly what you did."

He tried to rise to his feet, but Julian stepped toward him again. "Wait a second," Roman said, holding up his hand. "I have no idea why you're angry with me. Whatever it is you think I've done, surely it can be fixed. We're brothers."

Julian's eyes narrowed. "What you've done can't be undone."

Roman was about to respond when he heard the squeal of tires outside and a car door slamming. Seconds later, Shantel was standing in the doorway of the guesthouse.

What was she… Roman glanced up at Julian and it hit him. Julian must have learned he and Shantel had hooked up. But why was he acting like a jealous lover? If he wasn't mistaken, Julian had told him Shantel was like a sister to him. So why was he upset?

He watched Shantel survey the damage and turn to glare at Julian. "Why couldn't you have stayed out of this?"

"Because," Julian said, "he deserved that punch and so much more."

"Are you hurt?" Shantel asked, concern in her dark brown gaze as she looked Roman over.

After weeks of not seeing Shantel, Roman's gaze roamed over her as she walked toward him. But the woman coming toward him wasn't the same as he remembered. She looked tired, and her eyes were red-rimmed. *Has she been crying?* Was there some sort of lovers' quarrel between her and Julian? Is that why his brother came at him so hard?

Roman's stomach churned at the thought. He knew it was irrational to feel possessive about Shantel given they'd only been together the one time, but he was.

"No, I'm fine," he finally managed to say. "Nothing a bag of frozen peas won't remedy."

Shantel chuckled. "I doubt a single bachelor such as yourself even has frozen vegetables in the fridge."

But that didn't stop her from heading to his refrigerator to find out. After opening the freezer to search the contents, she turned around and held up some frozen peas. "I'm shocked."

She walked toward him, her hips swaying, and Roman couldn't help but watch. For some reason he couldn't put his finger on, Shantel did it for him even when she wasn't put together.

She handed him the bag of frozen peas and he pressed it to his jaw.

"Surprise, surprise." He grinned, and to his immense relief, he garnered a smile from Shantel.

Their gazes locked and held. Roman suspected they would have gone on staring at each other, but Julian coughed loudly. When he glanced in his direction, his brother still looked as if he was ready to thrash him.

"As much as I'd love to stay for the show, my work here is done. I did what I had to do." He turned to Shantel. "You need to tell him."

Shantel's eyes grew large. "You haven't told him?"

Told me what? Roman wondered, glancing at the two of them.

"No. You made it here before I could," Julian replied, "but now that you're here, you should tell him. I'm leaving." He started for the door, but spun on his heels to face Roman. "Know that you and I are going to have a talk when this is over."

Roman was completely in the dark about Julian's

ominous statement. Once the door closed, he immediately turned to Shantel. "Care to fill me in on whatever it is my brother thinks I need to know?"

"Can we sit first?" Shantel asked, and without waiting for his response, sagged into the sofa beside him.

"Looks like you need the rest more than me." Roman tossed the peas on the coffee table and came to settle beside her. "Can I get you anything? I have whiskey." When she furiously shook her head, he added, "Or I've got water, tea or juice."

"I'm pregnant."

Shantel blurted the words out. There was no other way to go about revealing the news she had to share but to get on with it. And once the news was out there, Roman's midnight eyes turned fiery.

"What did you say?"

"You heard me," Shantel responded. "I'm pregnant. And before you ask me if you're the father, the answer is a resounding yes. I'm not the sort of woman who sleeps around. You're the only man I've been with recently. So, there you have it. That's why Julian is upset with you."

Roman scrubbed his jaw and Shantel waited for him to say something. Anything. But then he shocked her by sweeping his strong arms around her and cradling her against his chest.

Shantel wanted to protest, to tell him to let her go, but she was overcome with emotion at his response. She didn't know if it was hormones or the fact that he was tall and powerful and larger than life, but she let out the tears she'd been holding in since she arrived. She didn't know if they were tears of sadness or tears of joy.

Now she was leaning towards the latter.

When she stopped sniffing, Roman drew back and looked at her and wiped her tears with the pads of his thumbs. "I'm sorry, Shantel. I'm sorry I haven't been there for you during this time."

"So you believe me?" she asked.

"Of course I do," Roman replied. "I could tell the night we were together you didn't take going to bed with me lightly. I should have walked away and let you go but I was so intrigued by you. I just couldn't, and well, here we are."

"Stop it!" Shantel said, pushing against his chest and putting some distance between them on the couch. Being this close, she was surrounded by his scent. Masculine. Provocative. It was all she could do not to melt into a puddle on the floor. "I want you and Julian to stop acting like I didn't have a say in what happened between us. It was *my choice*. I wanted to have sex with you."

But in her mind it hadn't been just sex. It felt as if they'd transcended the physical. Shantel had never felt such a heightened sense of attraction to another person. She'd dreamed about him. Replayed every moment of their lovemaking like a running loop in her head. The feeling of being out of control unnerved her because he was *more* than anything she'd ever experienced. She hadn't turned away from him then and she wasn't going to now. They would have to figure out how to move forward.

Roman's mouth curved into a smile. "I'm happy to hear that, Shantel, because quite frankly, after the night at the art gallery, I thought I'd taken advantage of you and you regretted our night together."

"I don't regret it."

"Even though you're pregnant?" Roman asked.

Shantel inhaled sharply. She hadn't known how she felt about the pregnancy until that moment, but she knew now. "Even then."

She was going to have this baby. She had absolutely no idea if her son or daughter might inherit her mother's illness, but she would do her damnedest by them if they did.

"When did you find out?"

"Over the weekend. I'd been having an upset stomach for a couple of weeks. I thought I had a bug or maybe even an ulcer. I was planning on going to the doctor, but my sister-in-law, who has three children, recognized the signs. She forced me to confront the truth by buying a home pregnancy test. Four of them, to be exact, and they all said the same thing. I'm going to be a mommy."

"Why do I feel there's a *but* coming up?" Roman asked.

"I wasn't ready to accept it," Shantel explained. "I guess I was hoping they were wrong, but the morning sickness didn't get any better. I've barely been able to keep any food down and today when Julian visited me at the office, I fainted."

"You fainted!" Roman was on his feet, starting to pace. "Are you okay? Is the baby okay?"

Shantel nodded. "I'm fine and the baby's fine. Julian rushed me to the ER, where they took a lot of tests, including a pregnancy test. I hadn't planned on telling Julian before you, honestly I didn't. But the doctor assumed he was the father and offered him his congratulations."

Roman nodded in understanding. "I see, and when

Julian figured out how far along you are, he deduced I was the father."

"Something like that. I told him to let me talk to you, but he was furious and wanted to confront you himself."

"Oh, he did that all right!"

"I'm sorry for causing friction between you." Shantel would hate it if she was the reason the brothers were at odds.

"No, I'm sorry you've been going through this alone, but from here on out, it's you and me," Roman said, sitting beside her again and squeezing her hand. He pressed one of her hands to his lips. "And we have to do what's best for the baby."

Her brow furrowed with confusion. She thought that's what she was doing now. In her opinion, he was taking the news in stride. Better than she'd thought for someone who'd learned his whole world had changed overnight.

"Marry me."

Nine

Roman heard Shantel's audible gasp when he gave her a slow, lazy perusal. He seemed unable to hide how deeply he was attracted to her. Hadn't it been that way since the moment he'd laid eyes on her?

Is that why he was taking such a huge leap of faith by asking her to marry him? He, Roman Lockett, who'd always shied away from commitment, was now offering marriage? It wasn't like they couldn't co-parent and raise their child separately. It was an option, but Roman couldn't imagine his child not being raised in a two-parent home like he and his siblings.

Or was there more to his proposal than he was willing to admit? He certainly couldn't deny Shantel meant more to him than a one-night stand. It's why he'd run from their hotel room. But he wasn't running now.

There could be a silver lining in all of this. He could have his child and Shantel too.

"You can't mean that," Shantel replied, balling her hands in her lap.

"I'm absolutely serious," Roman said, sliding off the couch to crouch in front of her, his hands on her knees. "We can't change what's happened, but we can do what's best for our baby."

"No." She shook her head adamantly. "It's not a good idea."

"Would you deny our child the chance to be raised by a mother and father in a two-parent home?"

"Of course not, but have you even given any thought to co-parenting? We don't have to get married."

"I don't want to be a single parent, not if I don't have to be. And I'm sure you don't want to be one, either. If we get married, our child will have both of us."

Shantel rose to her feet. "Stop bullying me. I can't think straight with you coming on so strong. You've flung the word *marriage* at me as if I'm a dog with a bone dangled in front of it. I'm not going to jump."

Roman was torn between anger and amusement. He'd never had someone speak like that to him before and wanted to both shake her and kiss her to make her comply. "You're already five weeks along," Roman said. "If we get married now and fudge the dates a bit, no one will ever now."

Her eyes were cold as ice when they focused on him. "We'll know. And I won't lie. I'm not ashamed."

"I get that. I do," Roman said. "But now that I know, I want to be by your side. I want to be a father to our child."

"How can you say things like this? Did you even want to be a parent?"

"Yes, of course...one day."

"See." She pointed at him when he hesitated. "You weren't ready."

"And neither were you," he retorted. "But here we are. I'm trying to make the best of things and you're fighting me every step of the way."

"Because you don't *love* me," Shantel shouted. She sat back on the couch and tears slid down her cheeks.

Roman was quiet for a moment as he studied her. Her lips were pressed together and pain shadowed her eyes. *So she is a romantic.* He'd had no idea, but then again, they hardly knew each other. Perhaps he should pump the breaks and take time to think about proposing marriage. They'd shared one amazing night and now they were bound together by the child they'd created. "I'm sorry, Shantel. I can't offer you love at this point." He wasn't sure if he would ever be able to because he'd never felt it for another person other than his family. "I admit I may not have a good track record, but I promise you I will be a good husband. An honorable one. I will treat you with respect and kindness, and I hope you can give me the same in return."

She sniffed and glanced up at him with wet lashes. "I want to believe you, but it's hard to take what you're saying at face value."

"Let my actions speak for themselves and if I fumble I will give you sole custody."

"You would do that?"

"Of course, because I want the best for our baby and that's having you full-time as its mother."

"And our baby, will you love him or her?"

"Yes." He certainly hoped so. He would give his child all the love and affection he'd never received from his own father.

She gulped. "All right."

"All right? You'll marry me?"

She nodded. "Yes, but first I need to know if there's anyone else."

His brow furrowed. "What do you mean?"

"Are you free of entanglements? There's no woman waiting in the wings?"

"I promise you I'm very much single and able to make the commitment to you. So if there are no further objections…" He moved toward her and she rose to her feet, allowing him to draw her into his embrace. It had been weeks since he'd held her. He could see everything now, her long black hair, her smooth brow and elegant cheekbones above beautifully sculpted lips. "Shantel…"

She looked up at him and the torrent of emotions she aroused in him couldn't be denied. For a moment, she stilled as if she too was breathing him in. His hands slid to her hips and she tensed, but didn't pull away.

It felt right to be so close to her. And so, with a slow descent, his mouth covered hers. She accepted his kiss. Her soft, slender body folded into his. Her full rounded breasts pressed against him and dear God, her sweet, generous mouth tasted of honey and nectar. One of his hands slipped around the nape of her neck so he could kiss her more fully, deeply.

And each kiss only created a wilder hunger for her. He reached upward and caressed her breasts through the thin material of her blouse, but Shantel freed herself from his embrace.

"Just because I agreed to marry you doesn't mean I'm going to fall into bed with you again."

"No?" His brow quirked.

"No," she repeated, and by the look in her eyes, she meant business. Roman didn't understand. *Why is she pushing me away when she'd wanted that kiss as much as I did?*

Things were happening too quickly. Shantel was used to order and routine. Her life was predictable and that was okay with her. After the unpredictable highs and lows she'd experienced as a child, she liked knowing what was going to happen each day. But suddenly, her entire life was headed off the rails. She was pregnant by Roman Lockett, of all people, and not only had she agreed to marry him, she'd let him kiss her after vowing that he'd never touch her again.

What is wrong with me?

Shantel wished she could blame it on the hormones, but she'd been susceptible to Roman from day one. She was attracted to him even though her mind told her to keep him at arm's length. So why had she agreed to marry him? Shantel told herself it was to give the baby a stable two-parent home, but was she doing this so she could have Roman all to herself?

If she were, could she really keep a man like Roman satisfied? Wouldn't it be better to stay platonic?

"How do you foresee this marriage going?" Roman asked, folding his arms across his chest. "Do you see it as just a formality for the child's sake? Because I don't. If we can't keep our hands off each other now, it's only going to get worse when we're in close proximity to each other."

"I hadn't really thought about marriage at all," Shantel said, her voice rising. "This whole day, this night has been a complete disaster. I came over here to stop Julian and tell you about the baby myself. I didn't have a thought beyond getting to you first."

"Okay, okay," Roman said, softening his voice. "You've been under a tremendous amount of stress today. And I don't want to add to it if my advances are unwanted."

She hadn't said that.

Hell, Shantel didn't know what she wanted. It certainly hadn't been marriage to one of Atlanta's most eligible bachelors. Everyone was going to think she'd gotten pregnant on purpose to trap him when that couldn't be further from the truth.

"What are you thinking?" he asked when she remained silent. "Because I can see the wheels of your mind turning."

"I'm thinking this has been a long day and I need to go home and rest." Shantel got to her feet.

"I understand and I'll give you some space."

"Thank you," Shantel replied. She was exhausted from the emotional upheaval of the day. "I'm leaving."

"All right." He let her go, but Shantel could see it was on sufferance, and soon she would have to pay the price for the one night she'd allowed herself to be free.

Roman released a long sigh. He'd been going crazy for over a month, recollecting every memory of their passionate encounter. And now, Shantel was pregnant with *his* baby.

There was no doubt in his mind that he was the father. Although she hadn't told him right off the bat, Shantel didn't strike him as vindictive. She would have told him, but of course Julian stuck his nose where it didn't belong.

His brother's angry outburst had precipitated Roman finding out the truth sooner, so he couldn't blame Julian. He was the one who'd taken Shantel to bed. This was his responsibility.

Roman didn't know if he should be overjoyed or shaking with fear. Although his father had recently mentioned giving him a grandchild, Roman wasn't certain if he would be happy or call him a screwup for letting something like this happen in the first place. His mother would welcome the news, though.

He might not know Shantel, but Roman was determined to make the best of the situation even if she had misgivings.

The next morning, Roman woke up groggy. He'd barely gotten any sleep after the gravity of what he'd just done last night sunk in. He also thought about how his father might view his rash actions and knew what he had to do. Pulling his phone from his pocket, Roman called his lawyer and filled him in on the details. He would draw up a prenuptial agreement and have it to him tomorrow before close of day. A prenup was a sensitive issue and Shantel could react negatively if she thought he viewed her as a gold digger, which was far from the truth. He didn't know her well, but he believed her to be a good person. She was willing to put her desires and wants aside to give their child the best start in life. He would explain it to her and hoped she would agree. Roman was prepared to offer Shantel generous terms, but the paperwork would make it clear she had no claim to the Atlanta Cougars, his birthright.

After he hung up with his lawyer, Roman felt better, but still unsettled. They couldn't very well get married without rings. He contacted the jeweler Preston Holmes to come to the Lockett estate and he was there within the hour.

Wearing a navy pinstripe suit, Preston was several inches shorter than him with pale skin and a buzz cut. He carried a suitcase chock full of the most exquisite rings Roman had ever seen.

Roman quickly scanned the rows of precious jewels until he laid eyes on a ring resembling a flower blossom. A brilliant diamond in the center was elegantly framed by a halo of smaller diamonds laid out like petals. It was simple yet elegant enough for Shantel. "I want that one."

"You sure you haven't thought about this before?" Preston inquired. "You seem to know exactly what you want. That ring is four and a half carats."

"I'm only getting married once. So nothing but the best will do. I'll get you Shantel's ring size tomorrow."

"Sure thing," Preston said, packing up his suitcase. "Your engagement is going to be quite a shock and have everyone's tongues wagging."

Roman shrugged. "What else is new?" He was used to the media's focus, and his engagement to an unknown was going to cause a ruckus. He would have to spin it as a love story for the ages. The only question was whether his intended would go along with the fairy tale.

Ten

"Pregnant." Vanessa stared back at Shantel open-mouthed from across the table as they had lunch at a local delicatessen the next day. "You're not pulling my leg or something?"

"Not at all," Shantel responded. "I wish it was all a dream, but it's not. I'm going to have a baby."

"Dear Lord." Vanessa crossed her heart. "Do you know who the baby's father is?"

Shantel frowned in annoyance. How could Vanessa even ask her that? She knew Shantel did not sleep around. "Of course I know his identity."

"I'm sorry, Shantel. I never expected this to happen to you of all people. Ms. Put-Together would never..." Her voice trailed off.

But despite it all, Shantel couldn't think of the tiny life growing inside her as a mistake. "It's crazy, right?"

Vanessa nodded. “When did you find out?”

Shantel filled Vanessa in on her hometown visit to McDonough, the pregnancy test and of course Julian’s reaction and her subsequent revelation to Roman. Her best friend’s eyes grew larger with every passing minute.

“Well, no wonder you’re a bit stressed. It’s been a trying time and you pride yourself on calmness and stability.”

“This is far from that, Nessa. And there’s more.”

Vanessa fanned her face with her hands, reached for her glass of water and gulped it down. “Lord, girl. I’m not sure my heart can take much more.”

“Well…” Shantel paused for several beats. “When Roman learned of my condition, he proposed and I agreed.”

“Ohmigod!” Vanessa’s hands flew to her mouth. “You’re going to marry Roman Lockett?”

Shantel nodded and glanced around to make sure no one heard Vanessa’s outburst. “I never imagined he’d ask me to marry him. I was as surprised as you are.”

“But you agreed.”

“He made a valid argument about our child growing up in a two-parent household and I want that for my baby.” She pressed her hand against her stomach.

“I know, Shantel, but this is huge. You hardly know the man except for the one night you spent together. Are you really prepared to make such a big commitment? I mean, you’ve always been a romantic. I assumed you would marry for love.”

“So did I, but… I want a stable home for my baby. One I didn’t have growing up with my mom and all her mental health issues." Shantel couldn't explain it, but she was prepared to do anything for her baby.

"And Roman? How do you feel about him?"

Shantel released a deep sigh. "We have incredible chemistry. Is that enough to build on? I don't know. I just want to offer my baby the very best start in life."

"What's next?"

"Roman suggested we get together for dinner tomorrow night," Shantel said, "to discuss the details." She'd been pleasantly surprised when he'd called this morning. He'd sounded like they were discussing business and Shantel hadn't known what to make of it other than he was as floored as she by the turn of events. She wondered if Roman had told his family yet. She sure hadn't told hers.

As if she was reading her mind, Vanessa asked, "Have you told your family?"

"No, not yet, but I will. Only my sister-in-law Charlene knows I'm pregnant because she was there when I took the home test."

"Four tests," Vanessa corrected her, as if Shantel could forget. Each time one of those blue lines indicated she was going to be a mother, Shantel had wanted to throw up, but after a few days, she was starting to make peace with her condition.

"I intend on telling them," Shantel explained, "but I would like to clear the air with Roman first. Figure out what *we* want to do before bringing my family into the picture. I'm sure he feels the same way."

"I wonder how his parents are going to take the news. They may have wanted him to marry someone from their social circle."

Shantel shrugged. “I can’t worry about what they’re going to think about me because it won’t change anything. I’m having their grandchild and they can either get on board or get off the train.”

Vanessa smiled broadly. “You go, girl. I’m so happy to see you being smart about this. I just worry about your impromptu decision to marry Roman Lockett. He’s a known player and hasn’t been without his share of ladies while you…”

“I know how woefully different I am from the women Roman is used to dating,” Shantel replied.

“Really? You don’t seem like you’re nervous.”

“Because if I don’t keep face, Vanessa, I might fall apart. And I refuse to do that. I’m not my mother.”

Instantly Vanessa reached across the table. “Of course you’re not, sweetie, and I didn’t mean to indicate you were. You’re a strong woman, Shantel, and capable of handling whatever life throws at you. I’m playing devil’s advocate so you know what you’re getting yourself into.”

“And I appreciate it, but I don’t need any more insecurities going into this marriage. My eyes are wide open.”

Or at least Shantel hoped they were.

Roman sat back in his chair and took stock of his life. He was in such a pickle. Tim Jackson had called him this morning and wanted to come visit Atlanta and meet his family next month before the draft. The last twenty-four hours had Roman in such a state, he’d completely forgotten about clinching a deal with Curtis. Usually he was focused on the prize, but right now Roman couldn't think about anyone other than himself.

He stared at the ceiling as Monday night's events came roaring back. His brother Julian clocking him in the jaw. Shantel rushing in to stop him from beating him up. Her shocking confession that she was carrying his baby. It seemed like a bad movie, but no, it was his life.

His one night of passion with Julian's friend would cost him his freedom. But what alternative was there? To be a single parent and be one of those see-you-on-the-weekend kind of dads? He wasn't knocking them, but Roman always envisioned being a hands-on father, someone who would be there for his son or daughter, offering advice and guidance. Someone who would listen and be supportive. He'd never felt like he'd gotten that from his own dad, so it was important to Roman. He supposed that's why he'd blurted out the marriage proposal to Shantel. It was instinctual.

And although he was nervous about the future, he didn't regret his decision. Given the same circumstances, he'd do it all over again. But they did need to talk through some critical items. Thankfully, his attorney had been able to courier over the legal documents this afternoon and Roman planned on giving them to Shantel tonight.

Once the matter of their finances was settled, Roman could finally tell his parents they were becoming grandparents and he was getting married.

He thought back to how his proposal hadn't exactly been romantic. He'd pretty much commanded Shantel to marry him and though she'd put up a valiant fight, in the end she'd known his solution was best.

They would become a family. The thought of Shantel's belly swelling with his child gave him a heady feeling and made Roman proud that another generation of Locketts would be born. He would not be deterred from the goal of making Shantel his wife.

And once she was, he would slowly work on lowering her guard so they could enjoy the off-the-charts chemistry they shared in the bedroom. Roman had no intention of having an in-name-only marriage. Theirs might be a marriage of convenience, but underneath it all there was a deep connection. He'd known it the night they were together.

Shantel wasn't like any other women. Was that why he was so willing to throw caution to the wind and marry her? He was still thinking about this when a knock sounded on his office door. His visitor didn't bother waiting for his response and walked right in.

"Julian."

He'd known they were due for a talk, but he wasn't looking forward to it. He acknowledged his brother as he walked toward him, but Julian didn't sit in one of the two chairs in front of Roman's large executive desk. Instead, he went over to the floor-to-ceiling windows and looked out at the playing field.

He was silent for several moments, so Roman waited.

When Julian finally turned around, scorn and derision were plastered across his features. "How could you?"

Roman wasn't going to play dumb like he didn't understand what his brother was talking about. "The attraction between us was mutual. It wasn't one-sided."

"You couldn't just walk away?" Julian asked. "Why

did you have to go and knock up one of my very best friends?"

Roman didn't have a quick comeback for that question. He hadn't actively gone looking to seduce Shantel. "We were both in the right place—"

"At the wrong time," Julian finished. "Shantel is a good girl. Is that what appealed to you? Her innocence?"

"Listen, Julian. I'm sorry you're upset. I wasn't intentionally keeping the night we spent together from you, but it was one night and I assumed—"

"She was like the other bimbos you date?"

Roman hated Julian finishing his sentences for him. It was a habit he'd had since they were boys. "Pot calling the kettle black," Roman warned, wagging his finger. Julian was as much a womanizer as Roman, if not more. His reputation was notorious.

"That may be so," Julian said, "but I've never crossed the line with one of your women."

Roman rose to his feet and stepped toward his brother until he was inches away from Julian's face. "Since when has Shantel been your woman? If I recall, your relationship has always been one of friendship. Or have you been keeping her in your back pocket in the hopes that one day when you were ready to settle down, you'd give her the time of day?"

"No." Julian shook his head. "It's not like that. I've never looked at her in that way."

"But you thought about it. For God's sake, if you can't be honest with your own brother, who can you be honest with?"

"Maybe," Julian said low under his breath. "Maybe."

"Maybe what?" Roman said.

Julian sighed wearily as if he had the weight of the world on his shoulders. "Maybe I thought one day if we were both still single, which in my ignorance I assumed we would be, since Shantel has never been keen on the whole idea of marriage and children, we'd see what happened."

"And now I've taken away your safety net," Roman supplied.

Julian snorted and his eyes narrowed. "Something like that."

"Well I'm sorry to tell you, Julian, that Shantel isn't *your* or anyone else's safety net. She's a beautiful, smart, sexy woman and she deserves someone who wants her for *her*. Not because she's their last resort."

"That's not fair," Julian replied. "And it's not like you've suddenly realized she was the woman you'd been waiting your whole life for."

"No, you're right." Roman could admit when he was wrong. "But I do want her. I have from the moment I saw her at the bachelor auction." When Julian began to speak, Roman put up his hand to halt him. "It's true, I didn't notice her before then, but I did at the event and we had an amazing time together. Our child is a result of that night and he or she is why I've asked Shantel to marry me."

"You did what!"

"C'mon, Julian, don't be selfish. You're upset because you wanted Shantel as your backup plan. Well, guess what? Life isn't all about you. I'm doing the right thing, what's best for Shantel and my child."

"Child?" a female voice said from behind them.

Roman swiveled on his heels and found Giana standing in the doorway of his office with her mouth wide open. "Gigi..."

"Did you say *child*? You," she pointed to Roman, "and Shantel? Are having a baby?" She shook her head. "Tell me I heard that wrong."

Why doesn't anyone around here knock? But when had the Locketts ever stood on ceremony?

Roman swiftly walked to the door, closing it and locking it. When he turned to Giana, both she and Julian were staring at him with perplexed expressions. "You didn't hear wrong, Giana. I'm going to be a father."

"I need to sit down for this." Giana headed over to a chair near his desk and plopped down, her dark hair flouncing as she went. She smoothed down the navy sheath she was wearing. "Please help me to understand what's happened."

"I don't intend on sharing the details of my love life with my siblings." His and Shantel's relationship was private.

"You sure as hell better be ready to answer our questions because once Daddy finds out, he's going to hit the roof!" Giana replied. "And Mama, she'll be happy as a lark. She's been harping about some grandkids for a minute. I'm happy you're the first to expect a stork delivery."

"Enough with the snipes," Roman said. "Both of you." He glanced at his brother. "I have enough on my plate as it is. Although Shantel agreed to marry me, it's far from a done deal."

"Meaning she could see the error of her ways and run for the hills?" Julian supplied.

Roman glared and Julian stopped talking. "There's

some unfinished business we need to address, which is why I've asked her to dinner, so we can talk through some of the finer points."

"Rome, this isn't some football deal you can strike up," Giana responded. "Surely you know that. You've asked this woman to marry you."

"I don't need my little sister to school me. I've got this."

Or at least he hoped he did, because everything hinged on Shantel signing those papers tonight. Only then would he feel able to move forward with the marriage. He hoped she saw things his way.

Eleven

"You look lovely tonight," Roman told Shantel once they'd arrived at Aria, a white-tablecloth restaurant serving American-style dishes in Buckhead. With its striking chandelier, modern art, metallic curtains and mirrored walls, the atmosphere was all glam. Of course Roman would take her someplace fancy. Shantel was surprised, however, when instead of being seated at one of the swanky tables, they were led downstairs to a cozy, candlelit wine cellar with a table set for two. This was definitely more her speed.

"Thank you," Shantel said, accepting the compliment Roman had given as she glanced over the five-star menu.

Shantel had tried her best to look sophisticated and elegant for the occasion. She'd chosen an off-the-shoulder emerald sheath and paired it with some asymmetrical strappy heels and chandelier earrings.

The waitress came over and offered wine. Shantel shook her head and when Roman started to turn it down, Shantel told him to go ahead and indulge. At least one of them would be able to relax.

This was their first date, after all. They'd shared a meal after the bachelor auction, but truth be told, that was all foreplay for the main event.

"Are you nervous?" Roman asked, glancing at her over the rim of his wineglass.

"A bit."

"You shouldn't be. We've been intimate."

"I know..." Shantel lowered her head.

"You really are a marvel." Roman peered at her as if she were some exotic creature he'd never laid eyes on. "I can see why Julian hates to lose you."

"Lose me?" Her brow furrowed. She had no idea what he meant.

"I... I only meant..." Roman stuttered, clearly at a loss for words, and put his wineglass down on the table.

"Julian never *had* me," Shantel replied stonily. "At least not in the way you're implying. We've always been friends."

"Just friends?"

"Yes. I adore your brother, I do, but Julian is a bit *too* much, if you get my drift. He and I would never work."

Roman smiled and she could see he liked her answer. She hadn't said it to please him, though. If she was honest, Julian and Roman were equally attractive, but Roman had that special something. She didn't know if it was his air of authority or his sexy swagger, but he spoke to Shantel on some elemental level.

"I'm glad to hear that," Roman said. "So tell me something about yourself. I know you're a psychiatrist who went to Spelman and came from a small town."

Shantel couldn't help but snicker because this really was rather awkward. They'd already put the cart before the horse, but hardly knew anything about each other.

The waitress returned to take their orders. Shantel went for the butter-braised lobster to start and scallops as her entrée while Roman opted for the Black Angus filet mignon.

"What do you want to know?" Shantel asked after the waitress departed.

"Tell me more about your family," Roman said. "I'm sure I'll be meeting them in the near future. Not to mention I need to have a conversation with your father."

Her brows furrowed in consternation. "You would do that?" Her father would appreciate the gesture, though he might think it was a little too late once he heard of her condition.

"Of course. I am a Southern gentleman." Roman's mouth split in a grin. "I recall you mentioning your father is a farmer?"

"Yes, he owns a three-hundred-acre farm in McDonough, Georgia. The farm has been in my family for generations. Along with our cattle operation, my brothers have helped my father develop it into an educational and agritourism farm."

"That's impressive," Roman said.

Shantel nodded. "It is. And my sisters-in-law have established a farmer's market and bakery where we can sell our produce. The bakery uses our strawberries, blackberries, blueberries and peaches in the pastries."

"So how did a farm girl like you end up in the big city?"

Shantel shrugged and gave Roman a whitewashed version of her life growing up. "I wanted more than the rural life had to offer," she responded. "And after seeing my mother struggle with mental illness, I wanted to help others."

"That's admirable, but why do I feel as if what I do for a living can never measure up?" Roman asked. "You *help* people."

"It's not a competition."

The waitress returned with their starters and Shantel dug into the delicious buttery lobster. She hadn't had much of an appetite these days, but tonight she did.

"I'm happy to see you eat," Roman said as she tucked into the dish.

Shantel glanced up from her meal. "I suppose most of the women you date probably have salads or move the food on their plate around without eating it."

Roman chuckled. "Who cares about them? Has there ever been someone special in your life?"

She figured they'd come to this part in the conversation eventually, but that didn't mean she was eager to revisit her past. "There was. His name was Bobby Winfield. We were teenage sweethearts."

"Let me guess, you went off to college and drifted apart?"

A lot more was involved in their decision to break up, but if that's what Roman wanted to believe, Shantel wasn't about to disabuse him of the notion. "Pretty much. And you, Roman? You're very eager to delve into my personal life but have avoided talking about yourself."

"You know my family."

"In passing, except for Julian," she replied. "You could tell me more."

"Okay." He leaned back in his seat to look at her. "My father, Josiah, is the patriarch in the family. He rules the roost with an iron fist. My mother, Angelique, is the long-suffering wife with the patience of a saint. Somehow she manages to see through his bluster because they've been married forty years."

"So you know what true love looks like, but yet at thirty-four you're unmarried. Why is that?"

Roman felt like he was one of Shantel's patients being interrogated on the sofa. "You sure don't pull any punches, do you?"

"I believe in being direct."

He was starting to like her even more. "I've never met a woman who intrigued me enough to take the leap. And before you interrupt me—" because he could see she was ready to barrage him with more questions "—there have been women whom I've dated, but I always managed to find something wrong with them."

"Were you looking for someone like your mother?"

He wagged his finger. "Oh no. Don't you go using your psychotherapy on me like I have some Oedipus complex. If I was opposed to marriage, I wouldn't be marrying you."

"*Au contraire.* You're only marrying me because I'm with child."

He laughed at the old-fashioned way she'd put it. "I'm marrying you because I want to. And because I want our child to have two full-time parents. I don't want to miss out on a moment of his or her life. Speaking of marriage, I need your ring size."

Shantel's mouth curved into a smile and it did something to his insides. He couldn't help it. He had a serious crush on this woman. If he had his way, they'd have forgone dinner and moved straight to dessert, but Shantel needed to be wooed. He suspected she wasn't comfortable with the idea of a marriage of convenience. He needed her to see it was best for everyone.

The waitress returned with Shantel's entrée of scallops, risotto and charred broccoli. His Angus filet was cooked perfectly and he enjoyed it and the crispy brussels sprouts and fingerling potatoes.

After she'd begun eating, Shantel took up the conversation where they'd left off. "I recognize the need for both parents in our child's life, so I'll tell you my ring size is a seven, but marriage is a big step. It's the joining of two lives. How is this going to work? For starters, where are we going to live?"

"At Lockett Manor, naturally."

"Naturally?" Shantel asked, dabbing her napkin on either side of her lips and placing it in her lap. "Why would we stay with your parents?"

"We wouldn't be staying with them. You know I have a four-bedroom home there."

"And you expect me to give up my cottage that I worked hard to purchase?"

"You can keep it as an investment and we'll rent it out."

"So my life changes, but yours stays the same? That hardly seems fair. I'm making the sacrifices, Roman. *I'm* having the baby. Now I'm supposed to give up my home. For what?"

He put his fork down. "For me. For our child."

"For you?" She whispered the words so hotly Roman was turned on, even though he could see from the way her eyes narrowed that she was blazing mad. "Your audacity is priceless. You think because you're Roman Lockett I should be honored you've offered to put a ring on it. Think again."

She didn't pause for a breath before continuing. "Let's be clear, shall we? *I* don't need you, Roman. I'm perfectly capable of raising this baby on my own. I'm *choosing* to set aside my misgivings and marry you, but don't get it twisted. You're not doing me a favor." She picked up her fork and continued her meal.

Roman was stunned. He didn't think he'd ever been spoken to in such a matter, but he realized she was right. He sounded condescending and uncompromising. Just like his father. It was no wonder she'd read him the riot act. But she hadn't become emotional and run away like most women. Instead, after presenting the facts, she'd politely resumed eating.

"I'm sorry." He wasn't used to saying those words. Hell, he wasn't used to being in a position where he couldn't make demands. It was her body. *Her choice.* And he should be happy to be along for the ride.

She flicked him a glance. "Apology accepted. But Roman, you have to understand, in order for this to work, there has to be a compromise on *both* our parts. I can't be the one doing all the giving."

"I hear you," he responded. "Have any suggestions?"

"I admit my two-bedroom cottage may be cute and quaint but not able to easily fit the three of us, but I'm also not sure I want stay in your home either. Perhaps we could find something that's *ours*?"

"Sounds fair." He hated compromise. His house was exactly the way he wanted it. He knew where everything was, but he also knew he had to give. "A friend of mine runs a real estate agency, I can engage him to start looking. Are there any areas of Atlanta you would prefer?"

When she smiled again, Roman's stomach eased. He hadn't realized how anxious he'd become thinking Shantel might back out. "Buckhead is nice."

"Okay, I'll get on it. Anything else?"

"I know you may want something big and grand because of your status, but I'd like someplace warm, homey."

"Duly noted." He picked up his wineglass and took a sip. "Why do I have a feeling I've barely touched the surface when it comes to getting to know you, Shantel?"

"What do you mean?"

"One minute you're the shy, unassuming woman I met at the auction. The next you're a fiercely independent mama bear. I'm trying to reconcile the two."

"Why can't I be both? There are many facets to me, as I'm sure there are to you. And I'd like to get to know you. Your hopes, your dreams, your likes and dislikes. So tell me, are you a cat or a dog person?"

"Neither. My father refused to get us a dog even though my siblings and I pleaded for one. He told us we wouldn't have time to take care of it."

"Then our child will definitely have one," she said with a grin.

Roman fell in love with her just a little bit in that moment.

"Sunrise or sunset?"

"I prefer sunrise," he responded. "I'm a morning person and like to get off to a good start."

"Hot dogs or hamburgers?"

"A nice juicy hamburger with lots of fixings is my speed," Roman said. "Now it's your turn. What motivates you to get out of bed every morning?"

"Knowing I'm being of service," Shantel said. "I find fulfilment in helping other people."

"You don't mind listening to their troubles?"

Shantel shook her head. "No, not if I can find the root cause. It usually stems from their childhood or a recent trauma. And you? Is being an executive of the Atlanta Cougars what you hoped it would be?"

"Yes and no."

"Explain."

"I like the power that comes from my position. I'm a good strategist, so being COO and director of player personnel plays to my strengths. My struggle is with my father. He refuses to let go of the reins. He wants to retain control."

"Sound familiar?" Shantel asked.

"What do you mean?"

"You're alike. You like to control things, as well. Have you tried talking to your father?"

"He doesn't talk. He dictates. It's only going to get worse once he hears about your condition. You'll see when you meet him."

"Is he old-school? Wouldn't he appreciate you stepping up and doing the honorable thing by marrying me?"

"Or he'll see it as yet another screwup because I can never please the man. You would think I would have earned his respect by now with all the hard work I've put in."

"Even if you haven't, you have to make your peace with him. Otherwise it will eat you up inside constantly trying to please him when he keeps raising the bar."

"You're very easy to talk to," Roman said. "I guess that's what makes you good at what you do." He'd shared more about his feelings with her than any other woman. Usually he was about physical satisfaction, and that was all.

How have I become so jaded? How had he not realized that he could have a deep relationship with a woman before? Was it because of Shantel herself? She was a breath of fresh air with a positive outlook on life, and over the course of the evening, the tension between them had eased.

There was no way he could bring up the prenuptial agreement tonight. It would ruin what had turned out to be a lovely evening. He prayed that when he did reveal his hand, Shantel wouldn't go running in the opposite direction.

Twelve

"Well, this is me," Shantel said when Roman walked her to the door of her cottage. She'd been surprised at how much she'd enjoyed his company now that the air of mystique surrounding him was gone. She had a better understanding of Roman, the man, and she didn't want him to leave.

The sexual magnetism between them was so strong, it seemed otherworldly, but she'd told Roman a physical relationship between them wasn't in the cards and he was respecting her wishes. *So why do I want him to make a move?*

Ask to come in, she silently pleaded. *Ask to come in.*

"I've seen you've safely home, so I'll get going," Roman said, and descended the cottage steps.

Shantel stopped him when he reached the sidewalk.

"Would you like to come in for coffee?" She knew it was a lame suggestion, but asking a man to stay for the night was not something she did or had ever done.

Roman grinned and she saw his gleaming white teeth even in the dark. "I would love some." He quickly climbed the stairs and joined her in the small foyer. She fumbled finding the light switch and Roman helped her by flicking it on. Then he backed her up against the door. "I'm going to kiss you, Shantel. Is that okay?"

She nodded her assent, her eyes fluttered closed and her mouth parted on a sigh of surrender when he lowered his head and kissed her.

God, it *was* as good as she remembered! Every female sense she possessed was on heightened alert. She clung to him, welcoming the feel of his taut body as he smothered her with the heated pressure of his mouth and obliterated all thought of anything but him.

Her lips parted readily and she welcomed the invasion of his tongue. She didn't complain when his hands stroked upward from her waist to mold her breasts, caressing them over her dress. Shantel wanted his hands and his mouth on her body. She wanted to feel the touch of his hot skin on hers.

Abruptly his lips left hers. "What are you doing to me, woman? You've got me in such a state, I could almost take you right here."

"And would that be such a bad thing?" Shantel could hardly believe the words coming from her own mouth, but for some reason, fate had set Roman in her path and she was done analyzing the situation like she usually did. She just wanted to feel.

He held out his hand to her. "Take me to your bedroom."

Shantel led him down the narrow hallway to the master bedroom. Years ago, the prior owner had combined two rooms to make a large bedroom, dressing room and en suite bathroom. She flicked the light switch and the bedside lamp came on.

It struck Shantel that she'd never had a man in her bedroom. Roman was the first. And he would soon be her husband, so it felt right.

"Shantel." When he said her name, his voice was thick and hot. A wave of desire clutched her stomach and her heart began pounding. She watched as he eased out of his dinner jacket and stripped off his shirt, then his shoes, pants and briefs. "Don't leave me in suspense," he said, smiling at her. "I want to see all of you."

Shantel unfastened the tiny hook and eye on her dress and slowly eased it down her hips. The dress fell away, revealing the curves of her breasts, which had been feeling fuller lately. She'd been unable to wear a bra and if the look of naked hunger in his eyes was anything to go by, he was happy she hadn't.

"Come here." He sat down on the bed and pulled her onto his lap. His hot mouth fastened over one nipple, sucking fiercely. Shantel arched her back against his arm while he explored the other breast in the same intimate detail. She felt his thick length underneath her bottom and couldn't wait to touch him, but he didn't let her. Instead he reached for her dampening thong and lightly traced her sex with the tip of his finger.

Her thighs trembled, but she didn't close them. She let him ease the thong down, inch by inch, and it was finally off. He tumbled her off his lap and onto the bed. They kissed deeply and madly, without reserve or restraint. Wet, hot, greedy lust took over and Shantel shamelessly rubbed herself against him. She needed to feel his shape and the scrape of his chest hair against her nipples.

"Jesus, Shantel," Roman said. "I intended to take it slow this time." She watched as he left the bed to source a condom and put it on. When he returned he said, "I know we're getting married soon and I'll take a test to assure you of my health, but until then, we should be safe, okay?"

"Okay and I'm safe too, but you need to forget slow," she murmured. "I want you now."

"Take what you want," Roman groaned, "but next time we do it my way."

He moved over her then and she guided him to where she wanted him most. He entered her with piercing sweetness and at first Shantel didn't dare move because she wasn't sure it was possible to feel bliss like this. Then he began thrusting with assurance and her whole body cried out with joy, but just as she was nearly hurtling over the edge, he hoisted her up and on top of him. Shantel had no choice but to wrap her legs around him. She wasn't used to this position. Naturally she adjusted her angle until she could take him fully inside her again.

She and Bobby had always done it the same way each time: in the missionary position. This seemed so much more intimate, but it felt good. And so she began riding him.

The scent of Shantel, the softness of her skin, gave Roman the feeling he'd left this earth and entered heaven. He ran his hands over her breasts and up her back, cupping her bottom as she rocked her pelvis against his.

He was spinning out of control. He wanted to step back and regroup, make the moment last longer, but Shantel was in charge. Her black hair tickled his skin and he found himself winding his hands through the silky strands and bringing her mouth down to his so he could kiss her deeply. He was caught in something elemental, lost in its grip. Shantel writhed above him. He heard her breathing hitch and knew she was getting closer. He placed a palm on her leg and slowly slid his hands up her slim, toned thighs until he came to where they were joined. When he reached the cleft of her sex, she was so wet, his mind nearly blanked.

He traced her wet warmth until he came to the nub of her secret place. He stroked her until she purred out his name. Hearing that caused him to pulse inside her, which only made her ride him harder, faster, locking her legs around his hips.

His hands left her moist center and he growled, tightening his hold on her. Her nipples brushed against him and all he could feel was a raw, primal need to possess her. It was foreign to him but he didn't take time to think about it. He gave in to the unrestrained emotions, grasping her by her hair and giving her a hard and hungry kiss. Her tongue came out and eagerly mated with his. She took all his breath as she demanded more, devouring him, and when he could no longer fight it, he gave her what she wanted. A bright gold light exploded in his head.

And then there was darkness.

* * *

Roman awoke in the morning to sunrise flickering through the window. Disoriented, he glanced around and didn't immediately recognize where he was. All he saw were frilly curtains the color of lilacs, and then he looked down at the bed and saw Shantel curled around him, one leg thrown over his.

Whenever he was with this woman, he continued to surprise himself. He normally never slept over unless he wanted to spend more time with a female, and in most cases he didn't. They were usually one-offs for physical release, but he wasn't able to keep Shantel at a distance like he did with most women. She required more of him and Roman found he was willing to step up to the challenge.

He did worry, however, that their relationship might change once he shared the news with his family. He didn't want anything to disrupt this happy medium they'd found. Shantel had been unwilling to consider a physical relationship between them but she'd realized last night that she was fighting a losing battle. Their connection was too powerful to be ignored.

He'd been respecting her wishes, but hadn't been happy about it. So he'd been thrilled when *she'd* accepted the intimacy between them. After last night, he hoped she knew the idea of a marriage without sex was impossible.

She stirred below him and her eyes opened. Then she glanced up. When she found his gaze on her, her lids fluttered downward. "Don't be shy, Shantel," he murmured. "We did what came naturally and it was beautiful."

Her eyes gleamed with approval and he could see she'd heard him. "I'm normally not that..."

"Demanding?" he offered.

She chuckled. "Yeah, it's hard to put into words, but sex was never like this with my ex."

Although he didn't like talking about another man while in bed with her, he was curious to know more. "What was it like?"

"Predictable. Routine." She covered her face with her hands, but he removed them so he could look into her luminous brown eyes, which didn't need the benefit of makeup to shine brightly. "I sound terrible."

"No, you don't. You're being honest about how you feel and I'm happy you shared that with me. I don't ever want our sex life to be predictable."

"Our sex life?" she repeated with a raised brow.

He laughed. "That's right," he said unabashedly. "Because there's going to be a lot more of that until your belly is swollen with my child."

"Really?"

"Oh, yeah, and if you recall, I promised you last night, when it was my turn, I was going to make love to you nice and slow." He reached for her, pulling her into his arms. "I'm about to make good on that promise."

They finally got up and showered *together*, then dressed and made their way to Shantel's small kitchen. With Roman standing in the middle of the room, the space felt tiny. Shantel did her best to focus on getting mugs from the cupboard for coffee because Roman said he couldn't start his day without it.

After the coffee percolated, she poured them each

a cup. She offered him flavored cream and sugar, but Roman declined. "I drink mine black."

"At the very least I need a flavored creamer," Shantel said, doctoring hers up with cream and sugar. She took a sip and noticed Roman glancing down at his watch. It was after eight o'clock and she wondered if he had someplace to be. "Is everything all right?"

He glanced up distractedly. "Yes, of course. I was thinking how I'm always in the office at 7:00 a.m. and usually the last one to leave."

"So you're a workaholic?"

"Admittedly so," he said, and took a drink of his coffee. "And up until now, I never had a reason to change, but if you're worried about what kind of husband and father I'll be, let me assure you I'll adjust my schedule to be there for you and the baby."

Had he read her mind? How else could he know that was exactly what she was thinking? Because she was her own boss, she was capable of switching her schedule to make room for the baby—and now *a husband.* "Thank you. I appreciate your candor."

"Then let me be frank," he said, putting down his mug. "There are a few things we need to take care of."

"Oh, yeah? And what might those be?"

She watched him reach inside his suit jacket and produce a black velvet box. He slid it across the table. "Open it."

Shantel sucked in a breath and looked up at him. His gaze captured hers and held it, and she felt something fierce course through her. She wasn't ready to give it a name, so she schooled her features and opened the box. Nestled inside was a beautiful diamond ring shaped like a flower. Tears clung to her lashes. "It's beautiful, Roman."

"Allow me." Roman eased the ring from the box and, grasping her left hand, slid it on her finger. "How's the fit?"

"Perfect." Shantel squeaked out the word. When had he done this? It had only been twenty-four hours and he'd produced a ring.

"Now our engagement is official," Roman said, "which brings me to the second matter we need to address. Telling our families."

"Ah." Shantel let out an audible sigh. She wasn't looking forward to that. She suspected her father might be disappointed in the way their marriage came about, but ultimately he would support her decision.

Roman's family was a wild card. She had no idea what to expect from the Locketts. On the few occasions she'd come into contact with Josiah Lockett, he'd been larger than life, and Shantel had kept her distance. Roman's mother had been warm and friendly. She hoped she would be the same once she heard their news.

"Which would you like to tackle first?" Roman said. "If I had my pick, I'd say your family. I could ask your father for your hand in marriage."

Shantel saw what he was doing. Avoidance. It was something she saw her patients do often. He would rather deal with the unknown than face his own demons with his family. She didn't let her patients take the easy way out and she wasn't about to let her fiancé do it either.

"No, we'll meet with your parents first. How about this weekend?"

Roman rolled his eyes upward. "I see who I'm dealing with now. You prefer to tackle the hardest issue head on. All right, we'll do it your way. I'll make the arrangements." He glanced down at his watch again. "I'm sorry, Shantel, but I really have to get going."

He rose to his feet. He came toward her, and unlike before, she didn't try to ignore the attraction they felt for each other. She welcomed the kiss he brushed across her lips, but it was over quickly.

He moved toward the kitchen doorway. "I'll call you later?"

"Yes. That's fine. I have patients until lunchtime and usually have my phone off, but I'll reply then."

"Okay, I look forward to it." He turned to leave, but then spun around to face her. "Shantel?"

"Yes."

"Last night was great and I can't wait for a repeat performance."

Shantel hadn't intended for their relationship to become intimate. She'd been certain keeping their relationship platonic was best, but her wayward body had other ideas. Now she'd gone and completely confused the arrangement and gotten more than she bargained for. Roman would probably expect that their marriage would include sex because she'd given him mixed messages. She'd never been able to separate love and sex. Would she be able to in this marriage?

Thirteen

Roman didn't tell his parents why he was calling a family meeting over dinner the next Saturday, only that everyone's attendance was required. His parents had been curious about his request, but agreed to host. Julian and Giana both knew what it was about and agreed to support him.

Roman even managed to reach his baby brother, Xavier, after several tries. Xavier indicated he was taking some much-needed time away to get his head on straight, but Roman wasn't buying it for a second.

This time of year was tough on Xavier, ever since the knee injury that had abruptly ended his career as an up-and-coming quarterback two years ago. No amount of therapy would heal him; he'd always walk with a slight limp and it crushed his spirit. When he'd learned the future he'd worked so hard for his entire life was over, the entire family thought he might be suicidal. He'd gotten better since then but it was still tough on him.

Roman shared his thoughts about Xavier with Shantel over dinner that evening when she invited him to her place. After opening a bottle of wine for him and sparkling cider for her, Shantel began making dinner. He watched her cut up vegetables for a salad while working on the main course, a rump roast.

He'd never had a woman cook him a meal before. Usually he took his women out or grabbed to-go from his favorite restaurant. He was enjoying the down-home approach Shantel brought to his life. He felt grounded despite the fact his whole life was about to change.

He was going to be a father and although he was scared at the thought of screwing up, with Shantel by his side, Roman felt like he could do anything. That was the positive effect she'd had on him.

"How did you get Xavier through it?" Shantel asked, breaking into his thoughts. Roman realized his brother was still the topic of conversation although he'd moved on in his head.

"At first he pushed us away. That's when my father stepped in and told Xavier he either had to go to therapy or get the hell out of the family."

Shantel frowned. "That was some tough love."

"It's the only kind Josiah Lockett knows how to give."

"And you? What did *you* do?" Shantel asked, getting glasses, plates and cutlery from the cupboard.

Roman sipped his wine. "I flew with him to this great clinic in Denver. They specialized in sports injuries as well as the mental health issues professional athletes face. Sure, Xavier ultimately recovered and was able to walk again, but every year around this time, he goes off like this and cuts himself off from the family."

"It's perfectly natural, Roman," Shantel said as she left the kitchen to set the dining room table for dinner. He followed her and leaned against the doorway. "He's grieving the life he once had. How long has it been?"

"Two years."

"Although he may have accepted what happened to him here," Shantel said, pointing to her temple, "he's struggling to accept it here." She patted her heart. "Give him time. He'll come around." She returned to the kitchen and took the roast out of the oven. Once it had rested properly, she sliced it against the grain, laid it out on a platter and garnished it with parsley. Then she scooped the roasted potatoes into a bowl. "Can you take these in for me?"

"Of course." He couldn't believe the spread she'd made for him without even breaking a sweat. She followed behind him with a large green salad and placed it on the table with the roast and potatoes.

"Hope you don't mind. I already tossed it with a balsamic vinaigrette in the kitchen."

"Not at all." He walked over and pulled out her chair. Once she was seated, he returned to sit across from her. "Shantel, thank you for all this." He glanced around the table. "Other than my mother, no one's ever really gone through the trouble to cook for me."

"You have to be willing to allow it, Roman."

He stared at her for several moments. Shantel was not only a good listener, but insightful. She forced Roman to delve deeper into the motivations behind his actions. He hadn't realized he was keeping women at arm's length. *Am I afraid of them getting too close? Maybe because they may not like the real me if they got to know me?*

"Let's eat, shall we?" he said, changing the subject. "This looks delicious." He reached for the platter of roast and loaded his plate along with helpings of potatoes and salad.

"Clearly this line of conversation makes you uncomfortable," Shantel replied, eyeing him knowingly. "So we'll drop it. I won't push."

He was uncomfortable.

And that scared him most of all.

"There's something else I've been meaning to discuss with you and could really use your help," Roman said, glad to be off the hook on more serious topics.

"Sure, whatever it is I'll do my best," she said, cutting a piece of roast and taking a bite.

"I have a rather important client, Tim Jackson, who I'm trying to woo in the hopes his son Curtis will sign with the Atlanta Cougars. He's going to be coming to town next month from LA and I would love it if you could maybe do that thing you do and make him feel more comfortable."

Shantel chuckled. "I'm not a miracle worker, Roman. If he's dead set on his son not coming to Atlanta, I'm not sure what else I can do."

"Trust me, you have a way with people. Of easing their minds. I mean, look at what you've done to me."

"Done to you?"

"Yeah, you have *me*, *me* of all people, talking about feelings. Trust me, your presence could go a long way in assuring Tim his son is in good hands with the Locketts."

She shook her head. "I'm not a Lockett."

"Not yet, but you will be. And I know meeting you will be a game changer."

"I suppose. I'll do what I can."

"Thank you, Shantel. Your support means a lot to me."

And it did. This woman was making him lose his famous self-control. In business, he was hard, cold steel, but Shantel had him opening up like the flower blossom ring she wore on her finger. *What more does she have in store for me?*

After finishing dinner, they retired to the living room, where they spent the rest of the evening going over their schedules. The real estate agent Roman had lined up already had houses for them to look at tomorrow. Thankfully, Shantel didn't have any weekend appointments. Then of course there was the pesky issue of setting a wedding date.

Shantel wanted something simple and quick, but Roman refused to shortchange her. By the end of the night, he had her agreeing to marry him in a month. She didn't see how it was possible to plan a wedding that fast, but Roman was determined, and told her to hire the wedding planner on Monday, price no object. Their families had just enough time to adjust their schedules while giving Shantel a wedding to remember.

She appreciated his attempts to romanticize the event, but Shantel didn't want to get confused. She knew why they were marrying. She was pregnant and there was no other reason. Yes, she found herself quickly becoming infatuated with the man who was her fiancé, but she needed to be careful not to lose sight of reality.

"Roman, I've changed my mind. I need to tell my father first," Shantel said.

Roman sat up straight. "If you think it's the right thing to do," he responded. "Can you call him?"

"Now? It's late."

"There's no time like the present."

Reluctantly, Shantel reached for her phone and dialed her father. He answered almost immediately. "Shantel, is everything okay?"

"Yes, of course. Why?"

"You usually don't call so late."

"Well…" She paused several beats. It wasn't every day you told your father you were knocked up and having a shotgun wedding.

"What is it, baby girl? You're making me nervous."

"I—" Shantel didn't get another word out because Roman took the phone from her. Shantel heard their one-sided conversation.

"Mr. Wilson. My name is Roman Lockett and I've been seeing your daughter." He glanced at Shantel. "Yes, sir, she's a wonderful woman, which is why I've asked Shantel to marry me." Another pause. "I recognize I should have spoken with you sooner and that I've done this backwards, but…"

Shantel placed her hand over Roman's. She shook her head and mouthed, "Don't tell him about the baby. I want to do that in person." He nodded his understanding and handed the phone back to Shantel.

"Hi, Daddy."

"I'm surprised by your sudden engagement, baby girl, but if this is what you want…" His voice trailed off.

"It is."

"Then I'd like to get to know Roman. Can you bring him to meet the family next weekend?"

"Of course."

"It's settled. I'll see you then. And Shantel?"

"Yes, Daddy?"

"I love you."

Shantel ended the call and found Roman staring at her.

"How did it go?"

"Better than expected. My father is shocked, but can't wait to meet you."

"I'm glad, but you're still tense," Roman stated. "Come here. Let me help ease your stress." He patted the sofa by him and began treating her to a foot rub, which eventually led to his hands skating up her thighs and bunching her dress at her hips. She no longer found it shameful to part her legs for him. Instead she allowed his hand greater access. When he tugged the material aside so his fingers could work magic, her eyes fluttered closed.

Instantly she moaned as his fingers stroked and his mouth teased. He always set her on fire. She felt *consumed* by it. Need washed over her as he made her wetter and way more vocal than she'd ever been.

"Ready?"

"Yes…" *I am beyond ready.*

Suddenly he rose, edging up so he could press his body close to hers. A shudder of delight ran through her as their bodies crushed against each other. Roman feasted on her lips, exploring them with such thoroughness she felt he knew them better than she did. And she let him, opening herself up, so he could slide his tongue inside her mouth. She was so caught up in the moment, she didn't realize he'd lowered his pants and put on protection until he was sliding inside her, filling her completely. He moved slowly, keeping her on the edge for a long time, until eventually she wrapped her legs around him and held him close.

Tension quickly began building inside her. Shantel let out a series of gasps and sighs as he increased the pace, bringing her closer and closer to an oblivion she couldn't contend with. Eventually she gave herself over to it, screwed her eyes tightly shut and screamed just as his body became rigid above her and he thrust one last time into her.

Her last thought was…she was still fully clothed.

The next morning, Roman took Shantel out for breakfast at a small diner specializing in biscuits and gravy. By the end of the meal, their bellies were full and they were ready to walk it off looking at houses. They took Roman's Maserati Levante to meet their real estate agent. John Summers had found a few listings that met both their criteria. It had to be close enough to the Atlanta Cougars corporate headquarters for Roman's work and close to Shantel's office. It should be in Buckhead but homey enough for Shantel.

When they pulled up to the first house, Roman was suitably impressed. It was a newly built five-bedroom, five-and-a-half-bath home with a light-filled open concept main level with twelve-foot ceilings and beautiful beams. It had a chef's kitchen, quartz waterfall counters and a huge master bedroom with his and hers closets. There were also laundry and flex rooms and oversize bedrooms with en suite bathrooms. In addition to a screened-in porch, there was a covered outdoor space with a motorized retractable roof. It was everything they would ever need. The price wasn't bad either.

"I don't know," Shantel said as they stood in the easy maintenance backyard. "It seems like so much space for three people."

"Once you have more children, you can fill it up," John replied.

Immediately Shantel's eyes shot to Roman's and he could see her concern in their depths. "Give us a minute, John, will you?"

"Of course. When you're ready, meet me in the driveway and we'll head to the next house." The real estate agent walked away to give them some privacy, checking his phone as he went.

"More children?"

"Do you want our baby to be an only child?" Roman asked, looking down at her. As soon as he said the words, he knew want he wanted. More children to fill up the house as the agent suggested. He'd always enjoyed having siblings and he wanted the same for his child.

"I guess I never really thought beyond *this* pregnancy."

He stared at her. "Perhaps you should."

She swallowed and turned away. He could see she was struggling with something, but she wasn't talking to him about it, which was more and more unusual. As they got to know each other better, Shantel had become an open book and didn't mind sharing her feelings. He supposed that's why he didn't like the distance he felt now. "What's wrong?"

"Nothing." But her voice sounded strained.

"There's definitely something," Roman replied, grasping her forearm and turning her to face him. "What is it? You can tell me. Don't you want more children with me?"

"I—I…" Her voice trailed off and it gutted him. He'd never thought about having another baby until it appeared Shantel was taking it off the table.

"All right, well, we should get back to it." Roman refused to show his disappointment. They would talk about it later when Shantel was ready to share her feelings. "We don't have much time to find a place. We have a million and one things to do to prepare for the wedding."

"Okay." She allowed him to lead her to the car and remained silent in her thoughts for much of the drive to the next location. Roman didn't know why he was so upset. It wasn't like they'd discussed more children; he'd sprung it on her with no preamble. She obviously needed time to adjust to the fact that their lives were changing and expanding to include more than just themselves. But it wasn't easy for him either. He was scared to death, but he was doing his best to make life as stress-free for her as possible.

Ten minutes later, he drove them to a private cul-de-sac in a much-sought-after area in Buckhead. Shantel was practically beaming at the two-story home with its brick facade and porch. “Can’t you picture having two rocking chairs out here?” she said.

After John led them through the double doors with glass inserts, Roman knew it was a wrap. The house had a large welcoming foyer, crown molding, wood floors, a sunny eat-in white kitchen and a paneled family room with a stone fireplace. The master suite with its large walk-in shower and soaking tub really seemed to speak to Shantel.

“This is wonderful,” she said, touching the porcelain tub. “I can picture myself taking a bubble bath.”

So could Roman. He imagined Shantel covered up in bubbles and felt his groin tighten. “John, show us the downstairs.”

Roman’s favorite feature was the terrace level. It would be great for entertaining with a large in-law suite, tile flooring, built-in wet bar and an extra-large family room with a fireplace that opened to the deck with a screened porch overlooking a heated pool.

Once they made it to the pool deck, Roman glanced at Shantel, and it was clear her decision was made. “We’ll take it, John. Make an offer.”

Fourteen

"Stop fidgeting, you look great!" Roman told Shantel after he'd helped her out of his car Saturday night and led her into the foyer of Lockett manor to the great room, where his family typically gathered. She looked sexy to him in her simple belted polka-dot dress. Roman wore all black. "You're not being led to slaughter."

"Are you sure about that? You already have a strained relationship with your father. And you want to tell him the news straightaway. Is it any wonder I'm nervous?"

"Don't be," Roman said. "And as for my father, the direct approach is best. No beating around the bush." He would protect her and wouldn't abide anyone hurting her. They'd spent the last few days getting to know each other even better in and out of bed. It's why he refused to bring up the prenup. Shantel had become more to him than just the mother of his child. He *liked* her. A lot. More than he'd thought he was capable of. Perhaps that's why he'd been drawn to her that night at the Bachelor Auction. She must have placed her trust in him too, because she'd given him a key to her cottage. It said a lot about the path their relationship was on.

When they got to the great room, they found Roman's father leaning against the mantel while his mother and Giana were speaking softly on the couch. They'd dressed for the occasion, his mother in a silk lounge-wear set and his sister in slacks and a cashmere sweater. Julian appeared to be largely ignoring everyone as he stood in the corner of the room on his phone. He was in his normal attire of a lightweight suit with no tie.

"Hello, everyone," Roman said as they entered. He gave Shantel's hand a gentle squeeze and smiled down at her.

"So great of you to finally join us," his father replied, standing up straight. "You're a half hour late."

"I'm sorry. That was my fault," Shantel replied. "I couldn't figure out what to wear."

His father's eyes narrowed on her. "And you are?"

Roman moved farther into the center of the room. "Mom, Dad, I'd like to introduce you to my fiancée, Shantel Wilson."

His mother's hand flew to her mouth while his father stared at him as if he'd sprouted two heads. "Your fiancée? Since when? And why is this the first time we're hearing about it?"

Before Roman could answer his questions, Josiah Lockett was heading straight for Shantel. He tilted his brow and looked at her discerningly. "Wait a minute, we've met you before, several times here at the house. You came with Julian." His father glanced over at Julian. "You're *Julian's* friend."

"And Roman's fiancée," Giana piped in.

Roman appreciated the assist, but bristled at the way his father emphasized his brother's name. Shantel must have sensed it because she patted Roman's arm before answering.

"Yes, we've met before. Julian and I have been *friends* for a number of years."

"So you're not one of his girls?" his father pressed.

Roman glanced down at Shantel. She'd blanched, but it was Julian to the rescue, and that only annoyed him further.

"No, Dad. Shantel and I have never dated, have we?" Julian sauntered over from the corner he'd been hiding in and came forward to press a kiss to both Shantel's cheeks. She offered a small smile. "For one thing, she'd never abide my womanizing ways. I suspect you want a one-woman man?"

"That's right." Roman wanted to wipe the smug smile from his brother's face. But he was going to have to live with Julian and Shantel's friendship and shared past. "And we are excited to share more news. Shantel is pregnant."

"Pregnant!" His mother jumped out of her seat and rushed over to pull Shantel into her arms. "But it's so sudden. You've only just got engaged."

"It's the reason they're getting married," his father interjected.

"Josiah!" She turned to her husband and the meaning of the glare she gave him was unmistakable: he'd better heel.

"Although this is a shock, a baby is such exciting news."

"If you say so," his father responded dryly. "Roman, I'd like a word with you privately."

Roman looked at Shantel. She wore a polite mask on her face, but he sensed her unease.

"Go on, darling." His mother shooed him towards the exit. "Shantel, Giana and I are going to have a chat."

Shantel smiled over at him so Roman reluctantly left the room to follow Julian into his father's study. Once the door was firmly closed, he turned on Roman.

"What the hell is going on?"

"It's as I told you out there." Roman inclined his head toward the door. "Shantel and I are getting married and having a baby. It should be happy news to you since you've been asking me to settle down."

"And you?" His father looked at Julian. "Do you have anything to say about this?"

Julian shrugged. "It's not my business to have a say. But to clear up any misconceptions, Roman didn't steal Shantel from me. Shantel is a grown woman and she can be with whomever she sees fit. She made her choice. And it's Roman. As for my friendship with her, although we've known each other for over a decade, I suspect my possessive brother over there—" he glanced in Roman's direction "—won't appreciate having another man so closely involved with his woman."

For the first time tonight, Roman smiled. He was genuinely proud of Julian after that speech because every word of it was true. Roman did feel territorial about Shantel; she was *his* woman whether she was ready to call herself that or not.

"All right," Josiah said. "Sounds like you both know what's up. But let's be real, shall we? The only reason you're marrying that girl is because she's having your baby."

"That might have been the case when I proposed to her," Roman said. "But I genuinely like Shantel."

"*Like* isn't *love*, son."

Roman glared at his father. "I'm aware of that, but it could blossom into love."

"You?" Julian asked. "Do love?" He began howling uncontrollably with laughter. "In what universe? You've never even attempted a serious relationship with a woman."

"Neither of you know what I'm capable of," Roman responded. He didn't even know until he'd met Shantel and she'd opened him up to a world of possibilities. And sure, they made him afraid because he'd never given his heart to another human being, but if there was anyone he was willing to give it to, it was Shantel.

When Roman's mother went to check on dinner, his sister, Giana, stayed with Shantel in the great room. "So, how are you doing?" Giana asked. "Daddy can come on a bit strong."

"Yes, he can be intimidating."

"He's really an old teddy bear."

"I'll take your word for it."

"But you and Roman," Giana began, "you were holding hands when you came in. It looks as if you've grown closer throughout all of this."

Shantel nodded. She hadn't yet talked to anyone about her growing feelings for Roman, not even Vanessa. It seemed so unreal that she could go from her boring life to this new one in Technicolor with Roman. *Is it too good to be true?*

"We have. What's the saying? Adversity builds character?"

Giana laughed. "If you say so. Anyway, since no one else has done it, I want to be the first to welcome you into the family. I'm so happy you're officially joining the Locketts because, quite frankly, Roman needs someone like you."

"Why do you say that?"

"Because Roman has always been like a tortoise's shell. Hard to break. Yet in the last week, you've broken down Roman's walls, and he seems more open and engaging than I've ever seen him."

"Really?" That knowledge made Shantel's heart swell. Was it possible she'd made a difference in his life so quickly?

"Yes, so whatever you're doing, keep it up," Giana said as the men rejoined them in the great room.

Roman immediately came to her side and Shantel instantly felt at ease. He had a way of making her feel safe, protected. *Cared for.*

Roman's lips brushed across her ear and he whispered, "You okay?"

"Yes." She nodded. "I'm good."

"Dinner is ready," Mrs. Lockett said from the doorway. "Please come. The chef has prepared a delicious treat tonight."

Shantel stood, and Roman linked arms with her and

led her to the beautiful dining room done in blue-grays with traditional regency-style furniture. From the champagne giltwood trim details to the upholstered dining room chairs, it screamed sophistication.

Roman held out Shantel's chair for her, then sat beside her. She waited for the twenty questions she knew were coming, and over the course of the meal, Roman's parents delivered. His father's questions were blunt and to the point. He quizzed her about where she came from, the farm business, her family and when he should expect to meet them.

"Mr. Jackson should be happy when he arrives next week," Mr. Lockett said, glancing in Roman's direction. "He'll get a chance to meet all of us and see that you're settling down."

"Was that a dig?" Roman asked from next to her, and Shantel patted his thigh. She didn't want World War III.

"No," his father replied, "I'm merely stating the obvious. You were a single man and now you're not. It might alleviate his concerns once he realizes you're a family man."

Good save, Mr. Lockett, Shantel thought.

Mrs. Lockett was much subtler in her approach. But when she asked when the wedding was and Shantel informed her it was in three weeks, his mother coughed loudly.

"I'm sorry, Mother," Roman said. "I know it seems sudden, but given Shantel's condition, we thought it best to move quickly and expeditiously."

"Anyone with a brain will know if she gives birth seven months later that she was knocked up when you married her."

"Josiah Lockett!" His mother rose to her feet. "A word, please."

"Angelique." Mr. Lockett's tone sounded humble, but Shantel didn't care. Tears pricked her eyes.

"Shantel, I'm sorry," Roman said. "Let's forgo dessert and head home."

Shantel was on her feet and pushing back her chair when Mr. and Mrs. Lockett returned from the kitchen.

"Please don't leave." Mrs. Lockett rushed toward her. She glanced back at her husband. "Josiah, don't you have something to say to Shantel?"

The older man ambled over to Shantel with his head hung low. "I'm sorry. I was unforgivably rude." He glanced at his wife of forty years. "My wife and I are very happy to have you as part of the family, and I'm sorry if I didn't make you feel that way this evening."

Shantel doubted he was used to apologizing any more than Roman. "Thank you. I accept your apology, but it's late and I find I'm tired quicker these days."

Mrs. Lockett reached for Shantel's hand. "Of course, dear. I'm sorry we kept you out so late. I know your mother is no longer with us, so please do let me know if I can be of assistance with the wedding or if there's anything you need to know about being a mother as I have four of my own."

Tears slid down Shantel's cheeks. Mrs. Lockett's offer meant everything. She leaned forward and wrapped her in a warm hug. "Thank you. I appreciate it."

"Anytime." Mrs. Lockett patted her back and released her.

"Thanks for dinner, Mom." Roman kissed his mother

on the cheek, shook his father's hand and then waved at his siblings on the way out.

Once they were safely in the car, Shantel let out a long sigh. "I'm glad that's over."

"You and me both." Roman was clutching the steering wheel.

"That was much harder than I thought it would be. I underestimated your father's animosity. I won't do that again."

"He's not angry with you, Shantel. I promise you," Roman said, turning to her. "It's me he's angry with. It's me he's disappointed in."

He could have fooled her, Shantel thought, but didn't poke the bear. She yawned and leaned back in the passenger seat.

"Looks like I need to get Sleeping Beauty home, but your house is a good forty-minute drive. Would you like to stay at my place? It's up the road."

"Sure, I'd like that." With their wedding a few weeks away, it was like they were on a speed-engagement and trying to get it all in. Yet with Roman at her side, Shantel felt all things were possible. She wouldn't have even thought it mere days ago when he'd thrown out the *M* word, but after getting to know him, she saw he was a man of deep principles, and she was slowly but surely falling in love with him each day.

Fifteen

Roman dropped Shantel off at her cottage the next morning. Shantel used her free time to check in with Vanessa from her car while running errands before meeting with the wedding planner.

"Ohmigod, where have you been?" Vanessa answered almost instantly. "I've been texting you the last couple of days, and I all I get is 'I'll call you later.' I've been dying to hear how everything's going with you and Roman."

"Surprisingly well," Shantel replied. "Except for last night's dinner with Roman's parents."

"Take it from the top," Vanessa said. "Last we spoke, you were going to have dinner with Roman and figure out this marriage. Then it's been crickets since then."

"Dinner was good," Shantel replied. "Roman realized I wasn't a pushover and wouldn't do exactly what he wanted. He learned the word *compromise*. We agreed not to live at his place on the Lockett estate as he assumed we would, but instead find a place that was ours."

"Wow! That is progress. Go on."

"It is. He lined up a real estate agent and oh, Vanessa, we found this beautiful two-story house yesterday in Buckhead. It's on a private cul-de-sac and it's perfect."

"You guys sure didn't waste any time."

Shantel laughed. "We can't. We're on a tight schedule with a baby coming soon."

"True, true. And the Locketts?"

"Roman arranged for dinner last night so we could tell his parents. Julian and Giana already knew. Apparently his sister overhead him and Julian talking."

"And his parents, how did they react?"

"His mother was wonderful. She's excited to be a grandma, but Josiah Lockett was a pistol."

"What did he do?"

"Oh, he grilled me over dinner about my entire life, my family. I'm surprised he didn't ask for my freaking blood type, because his questions ran the gamut. But it wasn't what he was asking, it was his delivery. He was very...antagonistic."

"I'm sorry. I suspected it wasn't going to be easy."

"I could handle him if it was a class issue," Shantel replied. "I don't know, I got the distinct impression he wasn't rooting for us like the rest of the family. I can see why he and Roman have a strained relationship. I don't know if our marriage and a grandchild will bridge the gap, but I'll do my best."

"Sounds like you've made your peace with the outcome."

"Don't have much choice in the matter," Shantel said. "I want my baby to have the very best in life, but there's more."

"What else could there be?"

"I'm falling for him, Nessa." Vanessa began to interrupt, but she continued, "I know. It's crazy. We haven't spent very much time together, but I can't help how I feel. Roman makes me weak in the knees."

"Does this mean—did you and he…?"

"We have." Shantel giggled. "Many times over."

"Are you sure you're not mixing up lust with love, Shantel? I mean, you haven't had a lot of lovers to compare Roman to."

Shantel understood why Vanessa would think that. Hell, she probably would too if she stepped back long enough to examine it, but she wasn't. For the first time, she was allowing feelings she'd always feared to develop. "You could be right, but I don't care. I love the place Roman and I are in. Is it wrong to be hopeful?"

"Of course not, and I don't want to take that away from you. I just hope he doesn't break your heart."

Shantel hoped the same, but there was no guarantee Roman was feeling the same way she did. It was a gamble to put her heart on the line not knowing how he felt, but if she didn't, wouldn't she regret not taking the risk at all?

Roman headed up to the main house and found his mother in the kitchen. She was arranging flowers in a vase on the large quartz island. "Hey, Mama, how are you?" He came toward her and brushed his lips across her cheeks. She was dressed casually in a tunic and palazzo pants, her always stylish hair in a bun.

"Darling," his mother answered, caressing his cheek. "Surprisingly well after your shocking news last night."

He stepped back and regarded her. "I'm sure it was, but there was no easy way to tell you."

"Oh, I agree." His mother stopped fiddling with the lilacs to look at him. "But surely you could have told us privately without all the fanfare."

"Would that change anything?" Roman said. "Dad was still going to have a coronary regardless."

"He only wants what's best for you."

"Then he should be happy for me." Roman raised his voice, but at his mother's reproachful look, he lowered it. "Why can't he be happy for me, Mama? I'm going to be a *father*."

Her eyes glistened with tears. "I know, and I worry for you."

"Why?"

"Because you've never said you wanted marriage, babies, any of it," she responded. "It's why we're both concerned that you're rushing into this. As much as I love the fact I'm going to be a grandma, surely you could coparent?"

"No." Roman refused to consider it. "I don't want to be a part-time father. I want to mold him or her."

"That's admirable!" His mother stared at him as if she was in awe. "I'm proud to see you stepping up, but what about Shantel?"

He frowned. "What about her?"

"Do you have feelings for Shantel? You were very

protective of her. I wondered if there could be more between you two."

"I… I…" Roman wanted to deny it, but he couldn't. He was developing strong feelings for the mother of his child. "Yes, I am."

"So your marriage isn't just about the baby?"

He stared at her and realized he'd never asked himself if there was another motivation for why he was so insistent on marrying Shantel. He only knew he *had* to have her. She was his woman. "No, the baby isn't the only reason I want to marry her. You saw for yourself last night, Mama. She's an amazing woman. She's not only beautiful, but she's smart and kind, considerate, thoughtful. She's going to be a great mother."

"And you—" she stepped toward him to cradle his face in her palms "—are going to make a great father. I'm so happy to see I was wrong. You also have a foundation to build on. It may not be love just yet." She stroked his wayward bushy eyebrows down. "But it'll get there."

His mother's words stayed with Roman after he'd left the house. *Love.* There it was. That word he couldn't seem to escape. He'd never been in love. He'd never even been close. At one time, he'd thought he was incapable of it other than the love he felt for his family, but maybe he'd short-changed himself. Perhaps love was in the cards for him, after all.

"So tell me, what kind of wedding do you want?" the wedding planner asked Shantel when she came to her cottage later that afternoon. Erica Shelton was a petite blonde in a killer designer pantsuit who got right to the point. "Big or small and intimate?"

"Definitely small and intimate," Shantel responded. "I'd like it to be family and close friends."

"Okay, great." Erica wrote in her notebook. "That tells me what we're working with, but we have a lot of decisions to make in a short time." She reached for her suitcase and opened it, showing her color swatches, catering menus, and photos of flowers and wedding dresses. "All right, I know all of this might seem overwhelming, but let me worry about the details. I need you to be high-level." She raised her hand above her head. "I've got the small stuff," she finished, bringing her hand lower, past her face.

Shantel let out a sigh of relief. "Okay, I can do that."

Over the next couple of hours, they narrowed down the overall color scheme, invitation design and flowers. Shantel opted for a spring look with a palette of bright blues, oranges and pinks. Their wedding cake would be an elegant tiered buttercream with orange and pink flowers. Erica had a location in mind near a lake with an attention-grabbing rotunda. When she showed Shantel the picture, Shantel knew it was the perfect location and hoped Roman would agree.

Erica left Shantel with homework—to find out if Roman wanted a religious or nondenominational ceremony, look over some of her favorite caterers' menus and select what type of music they wanted—and set up an appointment for her with a wedding dress designer for tomorrow evening. Erica would do the rest.

Shantel's mind was reeling as she walked Erica to

the door. “Thank you for everything. You’ve given me a lot to think about and I’ll get back to you.”

“Excellent. We’ll speak soon.” Erica waved and walked down the cottage steps to her car parked at the curb.

Shantel was closing the door when her cell phone rang. It was Roman. Her heart lurched at seeing his name on her display. “Hello?”

“Hello, beautiful. How did your afternoon with Erica go?”

“It went great. She really knows her stuff.” Shantel leaned against the door.

“Told you you had nothing to worry about. Erica planned a friend of mine’s wedding and they raved about her.”

“She gave us both some homework to do.”

“Oh, really?”

“If you’re free later, I need you to come over and have a look.” Shantel wasn’t going to be only one whose mind would spin. They were in this together.

“I’ll be right over.”

Roman didn’t know the first thing about planning a wedding, but wanted whatever made Shantel happy. When he arrived, she had a plethora of pictures and menus for him to look at. “You’ve been busy.”

She grinned mischievously. “Oh, you have no idea, but you will soon.” She rubbed her hands together in glee.

It didn’t take long for Roman to be deluged with decision-making. They had to decide whether they wanted a buffet or plated dinner? Open bar or beer and wine? Meat or fish? Eventually, they settled on hors d'oeuvres and a plated dinner with a top-of-the-line menu his mother would be proud of and a full open bar.

After calling Erica with their selections and making arrangements for a menu tasting, Roman and Shantel rewarded themselves with a bubble bath in Shantel's claw-foot tub. With his six-foot frame, it was a tight squeeze, but that made it even more enjoyable because there was nowhere for Shantel to go. He had his wicked way with her, kissing and touching every part of her he could reach. Afterwards, they retired to the bedroom, where he made love to her until they'd both worked up a sweat.

He rolled off her, panting as he stared at the ceiling. "What are you doing to me, woman?"

"I could ask you the same thing." Shantel turned on her side to face him. "You've made me into a sex addict." She wasn't even trying to reach for a cover anymore because she was comfortable being naked beside him.

He grinned. "Have I?" He was glad to hear he wasn't the only one feeling the maelstrom of emotions.

"I've never experienced anything like what we share," she revealed. "Before, I didn't know what I was missing so I could take it or leave it, but with you…" Her voice trailed off.

He flashed her a smile. He felt the same way. His appetite for her was huge and hard to satisfy. The fact that they shared this hunger for each other was immensely gratifying, but it wasn't easy for him to verbalize his feelings the way Shantel had.

Leaning over, he kissed her with a soft brush of his lips. Her gasp was soft and he kissed her again, his hands framing her face. He was lost in sensation and in the knowledge that he just might be in love with this woman.

He was surprised and a bit nervous at the prospect. He'd never been in love before, and had even thought himself incapable of loving another person. But in a short span of time Shantel was making him wish for a happily ever after.

Sixteen

The rest of the week sped by for Shantel. The purchase of the Buckhead home was in the works, plus there were tastings with the caterer and appointments with the wedding dress designer. By Friday, Shantel was happy with the progress being made considering the wedding was only two weeks away.

She thought about how her family would react when she told them her big news. Her father had asked that she bring Roman with her to the farm and promised a big Wilson family barbecue. Shantel told him not to go to any trouble, but he refused to listen. He knew this was monumental because Shantel hadn't been involved with anyone seriously since Bobby and now she was suddenly marrying Roman out of the blue. She hoped his reaction would be better than Mr. Lockett's when she revealed she was also having a baby.

Speaking of babies, hers wasn't settling down any time soon. She still had bouts of uncontrollable nausea. The meds her ob-gyn had prescribed had certainly helped, but they weren't a cure-all.

She'd been reading everything she could, including *What to Expect When You're Expecting.* She was surprised when she'd found a copy at Roman's place one evening earlier this week.

"You're not the only one going through this," he informed her. "I want to know what's coming next."

They spent most evenings together except tonight. Roman had a dinner with a sports agent and Shantel had begged off because she'd found herself more exhausted than usual.

It was nearly 10:00 p.m. when Roman called her. "How's my lady?"

The strong baritone of his voice wasn't the only reason warmth spread through her. He'd called her his lady. Surely that meant he was seeing her in terms other than the mother of his child, didn't it? "Sleepy," she responded.

"I'm sorry it's so late. The agent refused to give an inch so there was a lot of bartering going on. He wasn't happy we were trading his client for a younger athlete, but he's also representing another player we have our eye on, so he was lobbying hard on that deal."

"Sounds taxing."

"It was. I would come over, but I don't want to keep you up. Tomorrow is a big day."

"Are you worried?" Shantel asked.

"About meeting your father and three brothers? Hell

yeah I am," Roman answered. "I'm sure they don't want to lose the baby girl in the family."

"You'll do fine." Shantel knew for certain her father might be stern, but he was always fair.

"From your lips to God's ears," Roman said. He signed off several minutes later and Shantel sank back down into her plush comforter and fell asleep.

Once her family saw her with Roman, there was no doubt in her mind they would welcome him with open arms. Just as she had.

It was a two-hour drive from Atlanta to the small town of McDonough in the middle of the state. After they'd left the interstate, the roads had turned narrower and they'd passed by some small towns until eventually a sign read McDonough.

Along the way, Shantel told Roman about her family, all her brothers and sisters-in-law, nieces and nephews. Roman hoped they would like him. He hadn't gone to meet a woman's family and ask for her hand, so this was a big deal. He'd dressed with care in a silver shirt and pressed black slacks. "How do you think your father will react to meeting me after hearing about our engagement over the phone?" he asked. "Not to mention the baby."

Shantel wasn't showing yet. He was the only person who'd noticed how full her breasts had become.

She glanced at him. "My family is going to love you."

As soon as his Maserati Levante pulled up to the ranch-style farmhouse, Shantel's entire family piled out of the house to greet them. They plucked Shantel out of the car and into their outstretched arms while

Roman retrieved several bags filled with gifts for Shantel's nieces and nephews.

Roman watched as Shantel was gathered into the warm embrace of her family. It hit him how different their families were. Although his mother showed affection, Josiah was the exact opposite.

Everyone began speaking at once. Small children and a baby were being passed around so Shantel could hug and kiss each and every one of them. It was such a strange and foreign experience to be surrounded by such happiness and laughter. And love.

Her father stood back from the fray. He wasn't tall and athletic like his sons—he was short and somewhat portly—but he had Shantel's caramel coloring, brown eyes and broad smile. Shantel squealed with joy when she saw him and bounded into his arms.

"Baby girl," he said. "It's so good to have you home."

"Daddy." Shantel tilted her head to look at Roman. "I'd like you to meet Roman. My fiancé."

"Fiancé!" There was lots of whooping and hollering and back-slapping the likes of which Roman had never seen. But just like that, he was welcomed into the Wilson family because he was with Shantel. He could see they trusted her judgment implicitly. Roman was struck with how this meeting was nothing like his family's reception of Shantel.

"C'mon over here, son." George Wilson's hand was outstretched and Roman pumped it.

"Great to meet you, sir."

"Same here," Mr. Wilson replied. "You must have made quite the impression on my Shantel if she's willing to marry."

"Why is that?"

"After the way Bobby handled the news that we'd lost Shantel's mama, I thought she'd never marry." He walked towards the house, leaving Roman to follow and wonder exactly what her father meant and what Shantel hadn't revealed to him.

"He's the baby's father, isn't he?" Charlene asked, cornering Shantel in the kitchen when she went in search of a ginger ale to settle her quivering stomach. She kept crackers in her purse for moments like this when she felt a bit nauseated.

"Charlene..." she whispered, pulling her into the pantry. "Lower your voice. We haven't told the rest of the family yet."

"But he is the father?"

"Yes."

"I'm so glad he's doing the right thing by you, Shantel."

"I could have raised this baby by myself," Shantel stated, even though as the weeks passed she realized she wouldn't have wanted to. Having Roman by her side was much easier than going it alone.

"I know, Miss Independent. But two is always better than one," Charlene replied. "When are you going to tell everyone?"

"I was thinking after dinner," Shantel replied. She didn't want Roman to be grilled as she'd been by his family. Better everyone be in good spirits after having one of her sister-in-law's peach pies and homemade ice cream.

"All right, well, if you need anything let me know.

Christopher has already grown out of newborn outfits and is in clothes for one-to-three-month-olds now, so I've got plenty to spare."

Shantel smiled. It was hard to believe that in seven months, she too would be looking at baby clothes. "Thanks, Charlene. I might take you up on that."

The entire family sat down under a pergola decorated with twinkle lights in the backyard at a table filled with barbecue chicken, macaroni and cheese, collard greens, green beans with fatback, potato salad and huge jugs of sweet tea.

Roman couldn't ever remember feeling so comfortable and welcomed. Once everyone loaded their plates up with delicious goodness, her older brother Terrance asked Roman about the family business. "Tell us about the Atlanta Cougars," Terrance said as he dug into his plate of chicken. "Must be something, running a big football franchise."

Roman found himself talking about the history of the organization and how his father had purchased the team. He told them how each of his siblings played a major role in the franchise's success, but as the oldest he was groomed to take over. The Wilsons listened with rapt attention while they ate and drank sweet tea. Roman had never seen Shantel's eyes so bright. She looked happy. Content. He reached across the distance between them and squeezed her hand. She smiled, squeezing his back.

"I like it," Frank said. "As the oldest, you're heir apparent, yet you see it as a family business."

"Oh, most definitely," Roman said. "There's no *I*, only *we*."

The sound of a baby crying came from inside the house. “Excuse me.” Her sister-in-law Charlene left them to tend to the child. She was back a few minutes later with a tiny bundle in her arms.

“Oh, may I?” Shantel asked, eagerly jumping to her feet.

“Of course.” Charlene placed the boy in Shantel’s arms. “Say hello to your Auntie Shantel.”

Shantel’s eyes lit up when she looked at Christopher. She offered her finger, which the baby latched on to immediately. The sight of Shantel holding a baby who was practically a newborn was the most beautiful thing Roman had ever seen.

It made him think of how Shantel would look cradling their own child one day, and something inside him shifted. It was the tiniest of changes, but his throat closed up. Shantel was going to be an amazing mother, which made marrying her one of the easiest and best decisions he’d ever made.

Later, Shantel’s father came to Roman while the women were setting up dessert. “We need to have a talk, man to man.”

He glanced around for Shantel, but she was holding her nephew in her arms and paid Roman no mind. Although Roman was nervous, as any man would be asking a father for his daughter’s hand, he wasn’t afraid. Shantel said her father was a fair man.

They left everyone underneath the pergola, and George led him inside to the kitchen, where he pulled out a bottle of dark liquid and two shot glasses from the cupboard.

Both men sat down at the kitchen table. George poured them a hefty measure in each glass and handed one to Roman. "To Shantel," he said and they clinked glasses.

Roman threw his back easily and the fire of the whiskey burned all the way down. "Mr. Wilson…"

"Call me George."

"George, I'm sorry for not speaking to you first before asking Shantel to marry me, but Shantel's and my relationship isn't a normal one."

George sat up straighter.

"I only mean that it's unconventional," Roman amended at George's frown. "You see, Shantel is carrying my child."

George's eyes grew wide. "My baby is having a baby?"

Roman nodded. "Although I admit it's the reason I'm here asking for your blessing of this marriage, I have come to care a great deal for Shantel and I want the best for our baby."

"I can see that," George said. "It takes a brave man to stand in front of a father after the fact. I appreciate your honesty. Shantel's always had a good head on her shoulders, and if she agreed to this marriage, then you have my blessing."

"We do?" Roman couldn't hide his surprise. He'd thought George would be a lot harder on him.

"Yes," George said with a wide smile that smacked of his approval. "And we should drink to it." He leaned forward, removed the top from the bottle and poured two more hefty measures. "Here's to your marriage, my boy. May you and Shantel have a long life filled with love and happiness."

As he downed the shot, Roman thought about her

father's words on their union. He didn't just want a marriage of convenience. He wanted what Mr. Wilson wished for them, and he would do everything in his power to ensure that it happened.

Seventeen

The rest of the evening went swimmingly in Shantel's opinion. After disappearing with her father, Roman returned to the backyard pergola in good spirits. She walked toward him and he greeted her with a kiss. "I take it everything went well with my father?"

He grinned. "It went great! I told him about the baby too."

"You did?"

"Yes he did, Buttercup," her father said from behind Shantel.

She turned to face her father, one arm still wrapped around Roman. "So you're not mad at me?"

"How can I be mad at you, sweetheart? You're giving me another grandchild." He held out his arms to her and Shantel rushed into his waiting embrace.

"Thank you, Daddy. Your blessing means everything to me."

"I know it does, Buttercup, so let's tell everyone else." Her father clapped loudly and everyone stopped talking at once.

"Shantel and Roman have another announcement to make." He motioned the two of them towards the middle of the group.

Shantel looked at all the happy faces of her brothers and sisters-in-law and screamed, "We're having a baby!"

Soon they were all crowded around her, yelling and whooping with delight at yet another addition to the Wilson family.

As she and Roman settled into the guest room and slid between the sheets later that evening after the rest of her family had gone to their respective homes, Shantel couldn't have been happier. "You know, my father must really like you. He's letting you sleep in here with me."

"Considering your condition," Roman said, pulling her toward him, "I think the cat's out of the bag."

Shantel laughed. "Oh, Roman, I just love you." The second the words were out of her mouth, she recoiled, wanting to take them back. "I—I didn't mean that how it sounded." She tried to backpedal, but Roman's ebony gaze captured hers and he wasn't letting go. She tried to move away, but he held her steady.

"Hey…" He caressed her cheek when she looked down, unable to face him. "Look at me, please."

Shantel hazarded a glance at him and was surprised by his expression. It wasn't anger or even confusion.

She couldn't put her finger on the emotion in those dark eyes. She only knew she'd expected the worst.

"You've never lied to me before," Roman said, "so don't start now."

"I..." Shantel started to say she'd only meant it as a colloquialism, but if she was honest with herself, the words had been said so freely because it was how she truly felt. She loved Roman. But she had no idea how he felt about her. She supposed now she was going to find out. "I love you." She said those three little words again, testing them out for size. And waited.

"I can't say I'm exactly there yet," Roman said, and Shantel wanted to die. Then he added, "But I am falling for you, my sweet Shantel."

Shantel's heart swelled with joy because he wasn't casting her love aside. He was giving her hope. "Oh, Roman..."

They reached for each other at the same time and he kissed her so tenderly, she almost couldn't bear it. And when he stripped her naked, her senses flared because it was the way he touched her, the way he looked at her that made the tenderness so intense. She was bowled over by the way he leisurely stroked her body as if she was something he had to treat gingerly. And when he slowly pushed into her, she slid her hands down the strong muscles of his back. They wound their arms tightly around each other, lips locked as they gently moved together. His lovemaking was different—intimate—and it felt like love.

Tears started falling down her cheeks before Shantel was even aware of them. He must have felt them because his eyes shone tender and bright, but that didn't stop him from moving powerfully inside her until they rode over the crest together.

Afterward, he wiped her tears away with the pads of his thumbs. “Are you okay?”

She nodded. She was too afraid to speak for fear of sobbing. So instead, she slid to her side, and he pulled her to him until their hips were aligned. Then he draped one muscled arm across her waist. Shantel was glad Roman couldn’t see her face because she felt raw and vulnerable, more than she ever had in her life, and it frightened her. *What if my confession changes everything between us?*

Roman could still feel Shantel trembling beside him. He soothed her by smoothing his hand down her back until she quieted and he heard her breathing regulate. Only then did he lay his head back on the pillow and think about what had transpired.

Shantel loves me.

She’d said it. And he could have played along and let it slide, but for some reason he hadn’t been able to. He’d forced her to admit what she probably hadn’t been ready to. When she said those three words, there had been no mistaking her intent. And they made Roman feel like he was the luckiest man on the planet. It’s why he’d wanted to show her how much he cherished her, maybe even loved her, with gentle touches and soft strokes. He’d savored her as he had that first night, which seemed like a lifetime ago.

It had been intense, for sure, but he’d never thought it would keep getting better. Was it because there was emotion behind the action now? She wasn’t some ethereal beauty he'd encountered for one night. Instead she was the living, breathing epitome of his Mrs. Right. The woman he hadn't known he'd been waiting his whole life to find.

And now she was here in his bed, in his arms, about to have his child. Nothing, not money or power or prestige, seemed more important in this moment than what he'd just found with Shantel. So why couldn't he say those three words aloud? Because he was scared of truly letting go. He was used to being in control and when he was with her, he felt out of control. Was he capable of loving her the way she deserved to be loved, wholeheartedly without restraint? Roman wasn't so sure and so he remained silent.

The next morning, Shantel wanted to hide until she could analyze the situation and make sense of it in her head, but Roman wouldn't let her. He joined her in the small shower that morning, making sure she was thoroughly clean before he finally allowed her out. She'd dressed as quickly as she could and headed downstairs for coffee while he finished getting dressed.

Thankfully her father was out in the barn and she had a few minutes to pour herself a cup of coffee and *think*. So much had happened with Roman in such a short period, and in the cold light of day she was running scared. Roman had admitted he'd never been in love and was still guarded, while she had gotten swept away by lust, the wedding and everything in between.

"Hey, sweetheart. Where's your dad?"

And now he's using terms of endearment? Shantel

was getting everything she ever wanted but was afraid she'd never have.

"Barn," Shantel said, sipping her coffee.

Roman eyed her suspiciously and then joined her by the breakfast bar and poured himself a mug. "You feeling okay this morning?"

"Mmm-hmm." She wasn't known to answer in monosyllables, and Roman raised an eyebrow.

"If you're ready, we should probably get going soon. I have to get a few things prepared for the Jacksons' trip to Atlanta this week."

"That's right. You're hoping to show him Atlanta is the best place for his son."

"And that he's leaving his son in good hands with my family, *our family*," he amended. "You're still good with dinner with them on Friday night?"

"Oh, yes, I've cleared all my afternoon appointments."

Roman frowned. "I hope not on my account. I know how important your work is."

"I have another dress fitting and then I was splurging and getting my hair and makeup done. I want to look my best."

Roman placed the mug he'd been drinking from in the kitchen sink and sauntered over to her. "You always look your best." He touched the tip of her nose with his index finger. "You don't have to try so hard."

"I know. But I don't want to embarrass you." She still couldn't help feeling unease over his high-profile life and the need to keep up with the women he used to date.

"You won't. C'mon." He took her cup out of her hand

and added it to the dishes in the sink. "Let's get back home."

After saying goodbye to her dad amidst hugs and kisses, telling him they couldn't wait to see him at the wedding, Shantel and Roman left McDonough for Atlanta. They arrived before noon and Roman dropped her off at home, promising to stop by later.

Shantel was glad for a little distance so she could examine if she'd made a huge mistake by telling Roman she loved him. She recruited Vanessa to come over and help her pack because in no time, she and Roman would be moving in together at their home in Buckhead.

She shared her concerns with Vanessa. "What do you think?" Shantel asked after confiding how the evening went.

"Sounds like it went pretty close to perfect if you ask me," Vanessa said. "Your family liked Roman. Your dad gave his blessing, and on top of that, Roman said he's falling for you. I would say you're three for three."

"But he didn't actually say those three words like I did."

"Well, no, but give him time," Vanessa replied, closing up a box and taping the lid shut. "You two went headfirst into this marriage for the baby. Allow his heart to catch up to yours. Stop overthinking."

"I'm a psychiatrist, Nessa. That's what I do all day, every day."

"True, but you'll make yourself sick, wondering about the *what if*," Vanessa said as she assembled another box for Shantel to use. "And can you please tell me why we're packing? Can't your man find someone to do this for you?"

Shantel rolled her eyes. “I know Roman is wealthy, but I never want him to think I’m taking advantage.”

Vanessa put her hands on her hips. “You’re not taking advantage. You’re two months pregnant with his baby and isn’t the first trimester the hardest?”

Her question gave Shantel pause. She was right. “I suppose I could get a little help,” Shantel said, but she would pay for it with her own money. She and Roman hadn’t exactly talked finances yet and she was surprised by that. Hers were an open book; she didn’t have nearly as much as he did, but what was hers was his as far as she was concerned. *Does he feel the same way?*

“Tim and Curtis, welcome to my humble city,” Roman said, giving Curtis Jackson’s father a one-armed hug when he met them at the airport on Friday. He’d had a busy week at work and also got fitted for his wedding tuxedo.

It was hard to believe, but he would be a married man by next Saturday. Before, Roman might have feared tying himself to one woman who was so completely different from the aloof women he usually dated. Shantel was anything but; she was *very* accessible. She touched something deep inside him and he no longer felt in control like he usually did.

“I’m surprised you’re picking us up yourself,” the older Jackson said as Roman and Curtis placed their luggage in the back of Roman’s Maserati Levante. “I would have thought you’d have delegated the task to one of your subordinates.”

“Not at all,” Roman said. “You and your son are very important to me. I’m excited you’ve given me the chance to show you why the Atlanta Cougars is the team for your son."

"I've always liked ATL," Curtis replied, sliding into the back seat. "So many successful African Americans in one place."

"You'll love the close proximity to restaurants, retail and nightlife," Roman said as they pulled away from the airport.

"My son needs to stay away from nightlife. I don't want him getting caught up like some football players with drugs, alcohol and women."

"I understand that, Tim, but Atlanta is still a great place to live. It's a cosmopolitan hub with arts, history and culture, but it's also affordable. And let's not forget the weather. We have mild winters."

"You really are giving us the hard sell," Tim said. "So, where are you taking us?" he inquired, admitting defeat for now because Roman could go tit for tat all day.

"You'll be staying in the Presidential and Buckhead suites at the Waldorf in Buckhead."

"No need to waste good money," Tim replied, glancing in his direction. "My son and I can stay in one room. As long as there's a pullout sofa, I'm fine."

Roman knew better than to argue because he'd learned Tim would only dig in his heels. When they arrived he changed the reservation to one suite and left both men at the hotel to rest before dinner with him and Shantel later. Roman had a full itinerary to woo the Jacksons. After allowing Shantel to wow him with her charm, he was giving the Jacksons the red carpet treatment with a tour tomorrow of the Atlanta Cougars facility and an early dinner with the entire Lockett family, followed by a Drake concert.

He'd heard from a source that Curtis was a big fan, so he'd arranged for him to meet the superstar after the show. If this didn't convince Tim and his son the Atlanta Cougars was the team for him, along with one helluva contract, then Roman didn't know what would.

He returned to the office with enough time to wrap up some last-minute paperwork before showering in his private bathroom and getting ready for dinner.

Forty-five minutes later, Roman pulled up outside Shantel's cottage. She greeted him with a hug at the door. "I'm sorry I'm late, sweetheart. Traffic was terrible."

She looked sleek and sexy in a silk floral one-shoulder dress and embellished heels. All Roman could think about was taking her outfit off later.

"We should get going," Shantel said, locking her front door. He offered her his arm and led her to the car. She slid inside when he opened the door for her. He got a generous view of her thighs from the side slit of her dress. Closing the door, he quickly walked to the other side and started the engine.

"Traffic is dying down a bit, so we should still make our reservation," he said as they got on the road.

"How did it go with Tim and Curtis?"

Roman shrugged. "I put them up at one of the best hotels in Atlanta. Tonight we're taking them to one of the most expensive restaurants in town. And tomorrow, I've got quite the dog and pony show planned with the tour of the Cougars facility and the boys' night out complete with tickets to see Drake."

"The concert is great, but perhaps you might want to switch it up a bit for tonight's dinner."

"I don't understand."

"I'm just saying you're doing everything as expected. Wouldn't it be great if you tried something more authentic? They might appreciate it a whole lot more."

"With you dressed like a million bucks?" Roman asked. "You deserve a meal at the best restaurant in Atlanta."

"Humor me, will you?" Shantel asked. "What if you took him to some hole-in-the-wall place with good food and good music? Show him you're not a stuffy suit?"

At the stoplight, Roman turned to her. "You could be on to something. What would you suggest?"

"It's way out of your comfort zone and you'll have to lose the jacket and maybe roll up your sleeves and unbutton the top buttons of your shirt."

Roman laughed. "Wow, do I look that bad?"

"No, you're hot and you know it!" Shantel's eyes gleamed. "So, do you trust me to take you out of your comfort zone?"

"I trust you." And he did, more than anyone.

Shantel knew her idea to take Roman and his prospects to a local spot specializing in soul food with excellent blues performances was a risk, but she was certain if they saw Roman was more than the sum of his parts, they'd find he was the right person to sign with.

When they arrived at the hotel, the Jacksons were standing outside waiting. Shantel didn't hesitate to disembark, and instead of accepting the hand Tim Jackson offered, Shantel pulled him into a hug. "Tim, it's a pleasure to meet you."

Tim seemed stunned by her show of affection, but recovered quickly. He glanced at Roman and then back at her. "You as well, Ms. Wilson, but you didn't have to get out of the car."

"Nonsense, and call me Shantel." She came to the ambling football star. "And you. I can't quite reach you for a hug, so you're going to have to come down to my level."

"Yes, ma'am." He leaned down and briefly wrapped his arm around her.

"So, what fancy spot are you taking us to?" Tim asked once they'd climbed inside and pulled away from the driveway.

Shantel glanced at Roman and winked.

"Actually, Shantel thought you might enjoy a taste of Atlanta not many people get to experience, so if you're game, I'd like to veer off script."

"You're full of surprises, Lockett. But yeah, I'm game," Tim replied.

Thirty minutes later they pulled into a parking lot across from the local haunt Shantel had suggested.

Roman helped Shantel out of the car. "Follow me, gentlemen."

The foursome walked across the street and when he opened the door, Shantel could see the stunned expression on Roman's face as he took in the eclectic décor of the restaurant with its murals of blues legends and mismatched tables and chairs. This was so far out of his comfort zone, but he had his game face on. When the hostess came over, he said, "Four, please."

"Follow me." She led them to a small booth far enough from the stage that they'd be able to talk while the music played.

Once they were seated, Roman turned to Tim. "What do you think?"

Tim laughed and leaned back in his chair to regard Roman. "I have to give it to you, Rome. You're a man of contradictions. I never expected you to bring us to a place like this."

"How did you know that blues is my pop's favorite music?" Curtis asked. "He plays it all the time."

"A special someone gave me a suggestion." Roman rewarded Shantel with a warm smile she felt all the way down to her toes.

"You're lucky, Rome. She's definitely a keeper," Tim responded.

Shantel was tickled she'd gotten it right. Tim appreciated having a meal at a down-home place that happened to play blues. The rest of the night was straight out of Roman's playbook. He wooed Curtis and Tim with talk of the Atlanta Cougars while Shantel asked Tim questions about his family, his deceased wife and the future he envisioned for Curtis.

By the end of the night, Shantel was confident she'd helped the Jacksons see another side of not only Atlanta, but Roman. It had taken time for her to see through the facade Roman showed to everyone else, but if you pulled back the layers, there was so much more to him.

Her phone beeped and Shantel saw a text from Alma. She was pleading for a session tomorrow. Normally Shantel didn't do Saturday appointments, but Alma said she was desperate, so she relented and told her client she'd see her in the afternoon.

"Thank you so much for a lovely evening," Tim said when Shantel insisted on giving him a hug after they reached the Waldorf.

"Oh, absolutely. I had a great time. I hope you did, as well."

"Can't remember when I've enjoyed myself more. Shantel is a real asset to you, Roman." Tim shook Roman's hand.

The dark gaze Roman gave her made butterflies swarm in her belly. "Yes, she is."

"I could have used some hip-hop," Curtis replied. "I'm not really into old-school music like my pops."

Everyone laughed.

"Well, don't you worry, Curtis," Roman responded. "I've got a guys' night out with a concert tomorrow night."

"Oh, snap." Curtis gave Roman a one-armed hug. "Appreciate that, man."

"You're welcome. I'll see you both tomorrow, sometime after a late breakfast?"

"Oh, most def," Curtis said. "I have some jet lag so I intend to sleep in before I test out that stadium of yours."

"Look forward to it," Roman answered.

Once they were back in the car, Shantel was buckling her seat belt when Roman grasped both sides of her face and planted a hot and hungry kiss on her lips. When they finally separated, Shantel asked, "What was that for?"

"*That* was for making me think outside the box. You were my secret weapon tonight."

Shantel beamed with pride. "Glad I could help."

"You more than *helped.* You showed Tim I'm not some stuck-up rich kid. Thank you."

"You're welcome."

"When we get to your place, I intend to show you just how thankful I am."

Eighteen

"So, what do you think?" Roman asked after he, Giana and Julian had shown Tim Jackson around the billion-dollar custom complex. They'd returned to Roman's office while Curtis threw a couple of footballs on the practice field with the coaches he'd work with if he signed with the Atlanta Cougars.

"You've built quite the operation here," Tim said. "I'm impressed, but you are the Atlanta Cougars, after all."

"But it's about the people," Julian chimed in. "Your son would be in excellent hands. You saw the cutting-edge gym and weight room as well as the physical therapy and recovery areas, which I oversee. Curtis's health would be closely monitored by a team of professionals."

"I do like a family business."

"And I would work with Curtis and his agent to ensure the best deals come his way." Giana continued where Julian left off, tag-teaming the father. "We help our players build a brand because we want them to have a long, industrious career."

"Is all your family as eloquent as you and your wife?" Tim asked, looking at Roman. "Oh, my apologies, your fiancée."

Roman grinned. "No worries. She'll be my wife by next week."

"I really enjoyed her company," Tim said. "Will she be joining us this evening at your parents'?"

"Absolutely."

"All right, well, I'd like to go to the field with Curtis if you don't mind."

"Of course," Julian replied first. "I'll show you the way. I'm headed in that direction." He nodded at Roman as he led Tim out.

Once the door was shut, Roman couldn't resist kicking up a leg. "We have him on the ropes, Gigi. All we have to do is seal the deal tonight."

"What did Shantel do?" Giana asked, her eyes alight with joy. "You seem invigorated. I've never seen you so on top of your game like you were today."

"Giana, I can't explain it," Roman said. His head was still spinning from the experience. "Somehow she gave me new life with Tim. Made him see us with fresh eyes."

"I'm glad for you, Roman. Daddy is going to be thrilled."

"Don't jinx me. We're not there yet." Roman prayed tonight went off without a hitch because if it did, he was going to make some demands of his own to dear ole Dad.

* * *

After last night, Shantel should have been on cloud nine, but she wasn't. Alma's text concerned her, which was why she'd agreed to office hours on a Saturday afternoon when she had a million other things to do for the wedding, not to mention packing to move.

Shantel had no idea what Alma wanted to talk about. She and her husband were already sleeping in separate rooms and Shantel feared it had only gotten worse. The young woman was still struggling with her infertility. Shantel was certain their marriage could be salvaged if Alma accepted other alternatives like adoption or surrogacy.

Shantel clutched her stomach as it began whirling in the familiar pattern, which meant she might not hold down her lunch. She rushed to her en-suite bathroom and emptied the contents of her stomach. When that was over, Shantel brushed her teeth and rinsed her mouth with mouthwash. After wiping her mouth, she returned to her office. She didn't realize she'd left her office door open until she walked out of the bathroom and saw Alma's dejected expression.

"Alma?"

"You're pregnant, aren't you?" Alma asked, her eyes brimming with tears. "I know because I've lived through four pregnancies. Morning sickness, right?"

Shantel couldn't lie to her. If she did, it would be a breach of trust, but she knew hearing the news would devastate her patient. "Yes, I am."

Tears slid down Alma's pale skin. "How far along?"

"Seven weeks."

"Were you trying?"

"Alma..."

"I know you don't have to answer and I have no right to ask, but during our sessions I always got the distinct impression children weren't on your to-do list, Dr. Wilson. I mean, you're not even married." Her blue-gray eyes went to Shantel's left hand and she saw the engagement ring. "You're engaged!"

"I am. Alma, please sit down."

But her patient shook her head and remained standing. This was going from bad to worse. *Why, oh why didn't I close the door and lock my office before Alma's arrival?* Her stomach churned with anxiety.

"No. I want to know when you got engaged. Was it this past weekend?"

"No, it's been a couple of weeks."

"But you haven't been wearing a ring." Alma was quiet as she listened to Shantel's answers. "So if you weren't engaged before and you're only seven weeks, that means this pregnancy wasn't planned, was it, Dr. Wilson? You got pregnant by accident?"

"Yes, it was a surprise."

"Ohmigod!" Alma's hands flew to her face. "It's so unfair. I try to have a baby by putting my eggs and Brian's sperm in a petri dish and hope for a baby. But you, you get pregnant like that?" She snapped her fingers. "You didn't even want a baby, while I want one so badly."

Alma fell to her knees and wept, rocking back and forth. Shantel approached her, but Alma put up her hand to stop her. "Don't try to comfort me."

"Alma, I'm so sorry. I know how much this must hurt you."

Her patient glanced up at her and brushed away her tears. "You have no idea how I feel. To live in my shoes when you didn't even have to try and are blessed with a baby. Do you have any clue how lucky you are? That there are women like me, barren and unfulfilled?"

"Alma, please..." Shantel could feel her throat closing up as tears threatened to choke her because Alma's fragile control had finally snapped.

"I have to go." Slowly Alma got to her feet, ignoring Shantel's outstretched helping hand. "I don't want to see you again, Dr. Wilson. I can't. It would be too much." She started toward the door.

"I understand." Shantel swallowed the lump in her throat. She'd always known it was a possibility but she'd hoped it wouldn't turn out this way. "If you won't see me, please do get help. I'm worried about you."

"You don't need to worry," Alma said, turning her head. "You should focus on your baby and staying happy and healthy."

Seconds later, she was gone, leaving Shantel racked with guilt. She had the one thing Alma wanted most in the world—to be pregnant—and it had happened completely by accident. She should be able to cope with Alma's anger, but her client's mental health struck a chord with Shantel. She supposed it had to do with losing her mother. Alma reminded Shantel of her mother. Shantel feared it wouldn't take much to push Alma to do something drastic and Shantel would never want to be the cause, direct or indirect, of Alma harming herself. Taking a deep breath, Shantel tried to calm herself, but she couldn't prevent the trickle of tears that escaped down her cheeks.

* * *

Roman was worried. He'd been calling Shantel for hours and she hadn't picked up. He hoped she and the baby were okay. He dropped the Jacksons off at the hotel to freshen up and told them a car would pick them up while he went to fetch Shantel. Tim was onboard with him taking care of his woman and agreed to see him at the Lockett estate.

As soon as he was able, Roman rushed over to Shantel's cottage. He didn't bother ringing the doorbell. He used the key Shantel had given him and opened the door.

"Shantel? Sweetheart, where are you?" Roman called out. He rushed down the small corridor and found Shantel sitting on the bed. She was dressed, but her face was contorted with grief. Fear struck through Roman like a blade. "What is it? You're scaring me. Is it the baby?"

Shantel shook her head as she stared into space. "The baby's fine. I'm fine. Everything's fine."

"Then what? What's happened?"

Shantel looked at him and tears stained her cheeks. "One of my patients who's having trouble conceiving found out I was pregnant. It was terrible, Roman. She had a complete meltdown. I'd kept my condition from her because I didn't want to h-hurt her… God, I don't know why I'm being so emotional about this." Shantel sniffed into the Kleenex in her hand. "I—I never meant to cause her pain."

"Of course you didn't." Roman took both her hands in his. "It was a reflexive reaction. Deep down your patient has to know you only want what's best for her."

Shantel shook her head. "It sure didn't feel that way."

She turned to him. "If you could have seen the despair and hopelessness in her eyes… It makes me remember my mom and how despondent she could be. I don't want anything to happen to my patient." She lowered her head.

"It's okay." Roman wrapped her in his arms. He was just thankful she was all right. When he hadn't been able to reach her, he'd panicked, imagining the worst. "What can I do?"

"Nothing," Shantel said dejectedly. "And now neither can I. She fired me."

"No!"

"Told me she can't see me anymore. She doesn't want to watch me getting bigger and bigger each day while the hope of her having her own child dies with each passing day. And I don't understand it, Roman, I don't. I thought that after all these months I was getting through to her."

"I'm sorry this isn't the outcome you hoped for."

Shantel sighed. "Me too." She slid out of his embrace and rose to her feet. "I should get ready. Repair the damage to my face, if that's possible."

Roman grabbed her hand. "Are you sure you're up for dinner with my family tonight?" He searched her face. "You've had a rough day. Maybe you want to stay home and decompress?"

"I can't." Shantel shook her head. "I'm your wingman, or wing woman." She attempted a laugh. "We made such progress with the Jacksons. I don't want to lose that momentum. I'll get myself together. I promise. Give me fifteen minutes."

"Are you sure?"

She nodded, but Roman wasn't buying it. He'd read women were more emotional during pregnancy and today had been tough. Should he really put Shantel through tonight when his father wasn't her biggest fan? On the other hand, it would help to have someone in his corner and with whom Tim hit it off so spectacularly.

Roman didn't have to decide because right on the dot, Shantel emerged from the bathroom with her face and makeup intact. Roman's heart did a cartwheel in his chest—she looked beautiful, and the emotion he'd known was growing revealed itself. In that moment, Roman wanted to share it with her. To shout it from the rooftops.

"Are you ready?" Roman asked, holding out his arm.

"Indeed I am," Shantel said. "Let's go close the deal."

But Roman had another in mind right now—a deal that was a lifetime. Their marriage. He felt like the luckiest man in the world.

Nineteen

The dinner party was already underway when Shantel and Roman arrived at the Lockett estate an hour later. She felt terrible that she was the cause of their tardiness, but it had been unavoidable.

She was trying to put the events of the afternoon behind her and focus on the present. Roman needed her to be her sparkling self when she felt the exact opposite.

A uniformed butler greeted them when they walked in and led them down the hall to a salon where Roman's parents were holding court with Curtis, Tim, Julian and Giana.

"There you dears are." Mrs. Lockett came toward them when they entered. "I was starting to worry." She hugged Roman and Shantel.

"Sorry, Mama. We had a slight hiccup."

"I hope everything's all right." She looked between Roman and Shantel.

"Everything is fine, Mrs. Lockett," Shantel stated.

"Ah, there's the lady of the hour." Shantel heard a tenor voice behind her and spun around to find herself wrapped in a bear hug from Tim.

"Good to see you, Tim." Shantel put forth her best smile.

"You, as well," Tim said. "I was sharing with Josiah, here—" he motioned the patriarch of the family over "—how you and Roman took me to the best blues joint I'd been to in a long time, and the soul food was on point."

"I'm so glad you enjoyed it," Shantel replied.

"Immensely," Tim said. "Come talk to me about what else there is to do in town, should Curtis choose to sign with the Atlanta Cougars."

"Son, if I could have a word," Mr. Lockett said from behind her. Shantel turned around and didn't like the look that passed between him and Roman, but she allowed Tim to lead her away. *Is it my imagination or did Mr. Lockett seem angry with Roman? And am I the cause?*

"Why on God's green earth would you take one of the top draft picks and his father out to some seedy blues joint when I specifically asked you to take them someplace expensive?"

Roman resented the implication he'd done something wrong. "The spot wasn't seedy. Furthermore, Tim had a great time."

"Oh, did he? He's probably telling you that to your

face while he tells his friends back home that the Locketts can't even afford to buy him a good meal."

"You're overreacting."

"Like hell I am," his father roared. "You deliberately disobeyed me."

"Listen," Roman said, coming to stand in front of his father and looking him square in the eye. "This is my deal, not yours. I'm in charge of player personnel and if you don't like it, fire me. Tim had a ball last night and as for Curtis, I have him covered with a backstage pass at the Drake concert tonight. Tim was fine with it so long as we weren't hitting the clubs later."

"You think you know it all?" his father said, circling him. "You, who were born with a silver spoon in your mouth, while all my life I've had to work and scrape for everything I've ever achieved? Sometimes life isn't easy and this deal is far from closed."

"Is that why you don't respect me?" Roman asked, his eyes narrowing to really look at his father. Maybe he'd finally hit the nail on the head in terms of his father's issues with him. "Because I have done anything and everything you've ever asked of me. But it's never good enough, is it? I don't know why I even bother."

Roman turned on his heel to leave, but his father wouldn't let him have the last word.

"You've let a nobody, a backwoods country girl, come in here and get your nose wide open. The sex must be good because she got knocked up quick. Let me ask you something. Has she signed a prenup?"

Roman's nose flared and he spun around to face his father. "How dare you?"

"How dare I?" His father stormed toward him. "I

dare because *I* built the Atlanta Cougars while your mama was still wiping your ass. It's *my* company, *my* legacy, and I won't have some nobody come in and take what's mine. So I suggest you find some courage to make her sign those papers before your wedding. Otherwise, you will be cut out of my will. My company won't be divided and given to interlopers."

"This conversation is over."

Roman had heard enough. He was done trying to live up to the great Josiah Lockett's expectations. He was striking out on his own. He was more than ready. He had the business knowledge and acumen to lead any Fortune 500 company just as he led the Atlanta Cougars. If his father didn't realize his potential, he was missing out.

Prenup?

Roman had a prenup prepared? Shantel rushed away from the study door. After extricating herself from Tim, Shantel had gone in search of her fiancé. She suspected a showdown was occurring between father and son and hoped to do damage control, but now Shantel doubted the relationship between father and son could be repaired.

But what hurt most of all was that Roman hadn't stood up for her. Josiah Lockett had said terrible things about Shantel and Roman hadn't said a word. Hadn't defended her. Shantel covered her mouth and ran down the hall. She was nearly to the front door when she ran smack-dab into Julian.

"Shantel, what's wrong?" he asked, searching her face.

"I can't," she cried. "I need to go. Will you help me?"

Julian glanced down the hall and she could see fury rising in him. "What did Roman do?"

"Nothing! I have to get out of here, okay? Before Roman sees me. Is there a side entrance I can use?"

"Yes, follow me." Julian led Shantel through the kitchen, where the staff was busy preparing dinner, to the massive garage that housed all the family cars. When he flicked on the switch, there was a Rolls Royce, a Benz, a Porsche and a Ferrari. "Pick your poison."

"I'll take that one." She pointed to the Porsche. She felt like she could handle it without wrecking it. She would return it as soon as she could.

"Sure thing." Julian opened up the key box hanging on the wall and after rifling through several keys produced a set. "Here you go." He tossed them to her. "Are you sure you're okay to drive? Perhaps I should take you. You seem really upset."

But Shantel shook her head. "No, go back in there. Seal the deal. Get Roman that contract. Maybe then your father might finally be happy." She rushed over to the driver's seat, buckled up and started the ignition while Julian opened the garage door.

Shantel was about to put the car in gear when Roman suddenly appeared in the driveway and nearly scared her to death.

Roman couldn't let Shantel leave without talking to her. As he'd exited his father's office, he'd seen Shantel running down the hall. How much had she overhead of their conversation? Was that why she was running away? He didn't know, but Roman rushed after her, only to find her in Julian's arms. That angered him.

After everything they'd shared, Roman wanted Shantel to feel like she could come to him, tell *him* anything.

He turned to glare at Julian. "Get out!"

"Now wait just a second—" his brother began, but at the enraged look Roman was sure was on his face, he said, "Shantel, if you need anything, you know I'm a phone call away."

Roman wanted to throttle his brother, but instead faced his woman. He had to find out what she knew. Schooling his features, he walked toward her. "Shantel, please turn off the car."

"No."

He raised an eyebrow. "No?" She had a defiant look in her eye he hadn't seen in a long time. "We need to talk."

"*We* have nothing to discuss," she responded, looking straight ahead as if he weren't there. "I heard enough from your father."

So she *had* overhead their conversation. He prayed not all of it, because his father had been pretty brutal. How could he spin this? Change the trajectory? Salvage what they had?

"I'm sorry you heard those cruel things my father said, but you know, *you know*, I don't share his opinion! Furthermore, why in the hell were you going to Julian when you should be coming to me?"

"Really?" She turned off the ignition and jumped out of the car, slamming the driver's side door. "First of all, Julian and I have never crossed the line, so don't you dare bring him into this. This has nothing to do with him and everything do with *you*, Roman. You were the man who didn't stand up to your father. You were the one who didn't tell him he was wrong about me. That I'm not some nobody, some backwoods country opportunist who got knocked up on purpose to ensnare the great Roman Lockett and steal his family business right from under his nose."

Damn. Roman sucked in a breath. She'd heard it all. What could he say that would convince her of his true intentions, his heart? Should he tell her he loved her? That despite pulling the strings and convincing her to marry him, he'd fallen hopelessly in love with her? That he wanted to be married to her more than anything? He doubted she'd hear him. She was too angry to receive any words of love or comfort, so he had to go with honesty.

Unadulterated honesty.

"Okay, okay." Roman held up his hands. "I admit when I first met you, I was intent on protecting my place in the company and had my attorney prepare a prenuptial agreement."

"So you admit there is one?" Shantel asked, folding her arms across her chest. "Exactly when did you plan on sharing that with me? We've spent weeks together. You had plenty of opportunity. Instead, you let me overhear your father, *your father* of all people, talking about it?"

"I'm sorry, Shantel. What can I say? Every time I thought about discussing it with you, it didn't seem to be the right time or the right place."

"All those times we talked—" Shantel cocked her head to one side to glare at him "—all the times we made love and you held me afterwards in your arms, you couldn't tell me then?"

"No!" he yelled. "I couldn't shatter the fragile thread of a relationship we were building with talk of money and power and status, because that's all the prenup was about. Holding on to my power and place above my siblings."

"Did you ever intend to give it to me? Or were you waiting until the wedding day to ambush me with it?"

"I don't know," Roman answered as honestly as he could. "Because quite frankly, I hadn't thought about the prenup in weeks. We've been growing so close. It never crossed my mind."

Shantel shook her head. "So you left it to chance like a game of Russian roulette? This is my life, *our child's life*, we're talking about and you didn't think it was worthy of discussion? Let's be honest, Roman. You didn't expect this marriage to last. You expected us to fail."

"Shantel..."

"Admit it!" she screamed.

"Okay, at first, yes. I didn't think we had what it took. I thought we might stay married until the baby was of a certain age and then go our separate ways, but you have to realize my feelings have changed. We are well-suited to one another and I didn't want to let you go. It's why I didn't think about that prenup."

"And now?"

"And now what?"

She pointed towards the garage door. "I heard what your father said, Roman. If you don't get me to sign, he's cutting you off. You're done! Finished at the Atlanta Cougars."

"I don't care what he said."

"Bull." He watched as tears streamed down her

cheeks. "You can't tell me you're prepared to give up everything to be with me." Shantel flicked the tears away with her fingers. "You don't even *love* me."

"Don't put words in my mouth."

"I don't need to. You said them yourself. You *care* for me, and you may have allowed me to romanticize how we could be more by saying you were falling for me. And that was great, by the way. It kept me firmly under your spell. Kudos." She clapped her hands in applause. "Hook, line and sinker. I fell for it. But it was all a lie."

"That's not true." Roman shook his head and he made a move toward her, but Shantel retreated behind the car, putting a great distance between them as if there wasn't a big enough chasm already.

"It is. I was a fool to believe you would ever care for me, let alone love me. Hell, my own mother didn't love me enough to stay alive."

He frowned. "What are you saying?"

"I'm saying she killed herself, Roman, rather than be with me, my brothers and my father because I'm unlovable and you've certainly showed me she was right. There's something fundamentally wrong with me for believing you could love me someday. I've been living in a fairy tale."

She moved from the rear of the car and Roman reached her as she put her hand on the driver's side door handle. "Shantel, don't leave like this, please. I know you're hurt and angry with me because I didn't do enough to stand up to my father."

He hated the look of acceptance on her face. "It's okay, Roman, you can stop the act. You were marrying me for the baby and I came along with the package.

Well, guess what? I'm relieving you of your obligation. You don't have to worry about including me in your life any longer. My baby and I are going to be okay."

"Don't say that, Shantel." But she was already pushing past him and climbing into the driver's seat. "We can get through this. Figure it out. If you'll just give me a chance to explain. Please don't leave. You shouldn't even be driving in this condition."

Shantel wiped her face with the back of her hand. "Oh, don't you worry. I'll be okay. I lost my mother and my first love left me, so I know how to cope with loss and I'll do it again." She started the engine and the car began moving.

Roman didn't want to get out of the way, but if he didn't she'd run over his feet. He stepped backward. "Shantel, please..." But his words were in the wind because the Porsche was already headed down the driveway, taking his baby and the woman he loved out of his life. Possibly forever.

Twenty

"It was all a lie," Shantel cried into Vanessa's arms as they lay in Vanessa's queen-size bed at her condo. Shantel hadn't even taken off her dress. Instead, Vanessa had helped her climb underneath the fluffy blanket and gotten in beside her, wrapping her arms around Shantel. "How could I have been so stupid?"

She'd called her best friend as she drove away from the Locketts' mansion. Vanessa told her to come to her place instead of going home, which was the scene where Shantel had unequivocally fallen in love with Roman Lockett.

"You weren't stupid," Vanessa said. "You were trusting. You believed every word Roman told you. There's nothing wrong with believing in people, Shantel. It's one of your great qualities and what makes you you."

Shantel glanced up and smiled at Vanessa through her tears. “If you could have heard the hateful things his father said about me.” She shook her head in amazement. She still couldn’t believe them. She’d stood there frozen in shock because the man she loved hadn’t defended her. Instead, he’d allowed Josiah Lockett to speak ill of her. “What did I do to deserve that? I’ve been supportive, helping him win over his prospective player. And yet he couldn’t come to my defense when the going got tough.”

“It’s unconscionable,” Vanessa said. “You shouldn’t have had to go through that. You deserve better, Shantel. So much better.”

Shantel nodded. “I didn’t deserve to be treated this way by someone who claims to care for me. That’s what hurts the most.”

“I know it may be too soon to ask, but what are you going to do? It’s not like you can just break up with him and avoid him. You’re having *his* baby.”

“I know,” Shantel cried. She’d thought about nothing else on the drive over. Her palm instantly came to rest on the light swell of her stomach. It wasn’t much but she was starting to see subtle changes in her body, which made this so difficult. She was carrying the baby of a man she was very much in love with, but who didn’t love her back or respect her enough to take a stand with his father.

Roman would forever live in Josiah’s shadow if he didn’t nip his father’s dictating ways in the bud. But he had been obeying his father so long, Shantel doubted he even knew how to break free, and she certainly wasn’t sticking around to find out. After losing her mother during those crucial teenage years, it was important to her that her baby grow up with two loving parents. Somehow, some way she had to figure out how to coparent with Roman without destroying herself in the process.

Several days later, Roman sat staring at the walls of his office. How was it possible that one thing in his life could go so perfectly while the other went off the rails in spectacular fashion?

He'd finally convinced Curtis and his father, Tim, that signing with the Atlanta Cougars would be a good move. Father and son were happy with the signing bonus and contract presented and were flying back home so Curtis could finish out his senior year. Curtis was determined his son would have a college degree.

And the person Roman had to thank most, Shantel, no longer wanted anything to do with him. She'd cut him off entirely from her life as if the last few weeks hadn't existed. But they had. If anyone had told him a month ago he would fall in love with Shantel and the tiny life they'd created after a moment of unforgettable passion, he would have called them a liar.

Yet that's exactly what happened. He'd fallen for her smile, natural beauty, down-to-earth charm and positive outlook on life. Because of her, he'd reevaluated his weekend with the Jacksons and she'd been right. Tim wanted to ensure his son wasn't another number, but would be cared for by the Locketts like a member of the family. And he'd gotten that.

Upon hearing she was ill, Tim had been disappointed not to get to say goodbye to Shantel. Roman had had to think quick on his feet when she hadn't returned with him to the salon the night of the dinner party. He'd revealed she was expecting and told Tim she was feeling unwell. Tim completely understood and Roman promised to give her his regards.

But now that the deal was signed, Roman felt numb. He should be celebrating. He'd pulled off signing one of the best wide receivers in college football to the Atlanta Cougars. He'd shown his father he was a man to be reckoned with. The win, however, felt hollow. He didn't feel right because it had come at the expense of losing Shantel.

She believed Roman cared more about business, power and status than their budding relationship. That would have been true of the Roman of yesteryear, but he'd changed since learning he was going to be a father. He'd realized nothing was more important than the happiness and well-being of his child.

There was a knock at the door and Julian hesitantly poked his head in. Roman couldn't believe he was actually respecting his privacy. "C'mon in." Roman motioned for him to enter.

Julian walked toward him with purpose and sat down in the chair facing Roman. He was silent as he stared Roman down.

"What?" Roman asked.

"Tell me you're not this daft," Julian replied. "Tell me you know you messed up and you're going to fight for my girl."

Roman's mouth turned to a grim line at Julian's use of *my girl*.

Julian held up his hand. "Don't even start. It's a turn

of phrase. I've been waiting for you to get off your butt and do something."

"What would you have me do?" Roman asked. "She refuses to take my calls, doesn't return my texts. She's blocked me."

"Then show up at her house. Convince her she's made a mistake."

"Been there. Done that," Roman said, standing up. "I went over to her house two days ago. She wasn't there. Not only was the place locked up tight, but she had the locks changed. My key wouldn't work. I even showed up at her office and her partner said she was taking a couple of weeks off."

Julian leaned back in his chair and regarded him. "Oh, she's really mad at you."

Roman shook his head. "It's more than that. She's disappointed in me."

"Why?"

"You mean, *your girl* didn't tell you?" Roman was surprised by that. He'd assumed Shantel had spilled the beans the night of the party when Julian had lent her the keys to the Porsche—which she'd sent back, shiny and as good as new the following day. Not a scratch on it. Any other woman might have thought to key it in revenge, but not Shantel. She wasn't built that way.

"No, why would you think that?" Julian stared at him and shook his head. "When will you get it, Roman? Shantel and I aren't down like that. Sure, we're friends, but she would never confide in me about something personal in your relationship. If she did, it might jeopardize ours, and she would never want that. You have to get over this jealousy."

"It's not so much jealousy. It's more of a proprietary feeling." At Julian's incredulous look, Roman continued. "I know it's crazy, but I feel like since we were together, she was my woman. And I know I didn't do right by her after our first night together, but since I found out about the baby, I've done my very best."

Julian nodded. "I agree. Even I was impressed with how you've treated her and I see she cares for you a great deal."

"She told me she loved me," Roman blurted out.

His brother's eyes widened in alarm. "She did? So what went wrong? It would have to be pretty big for her to walk out on you and cut off all communication with you and me."

"With you too?"

"Yep, I've tried. Calls. Texts. And no response."

She could be anywhere by now.

"So, I'm waiting," Julian prompted him. "What did you do?"

"I didn't stand up and defend her and her character when our father went off on one of his infamous rants. She heard everything. Every unsatisfactory thing our father said or called her."

"Lord!" Julian rubbed his head. "This is a mess. You need to find her, Roman. Tell her you're sorry. Beg and plead for her forgiveness, because I've got to tell you, you're not going to find another woman like her. She's one in a million."

"How can I apologize? How can I make things right if I don't know where she is?"

Julian released a long sigh. "Knowing Shantel, she

would go someplace where she would feel loved. Cared for. She would go…"

"Home to McDonough," Roman finished. *How have I not thought about that?* He'd seen the love surrounding her there with his very own eyes. She would want the comfort, security and love her family provided.

"Thanks, Julian." Roman came toward him, pulling him into a brotherly hug. "I appreciate you hearing me out and not jumping to conclusions."

"You mean like when I sucker-punched you in the jaw?" Julian laughed as the two men separated.

"Something like that." He began walking backwards to the door. "But I promise you. I will fix this and I will bring Shantel back."

"You'd better or you'll have me to contend with," Julian warned.

"Oh, I know, I know." He had his work cut out for him. Was there a chance Shantel would forgive him? Roman sure hoped so because he was banking his entire future on it.

"You sure you're okay?" Shantel's father asked her later that afternoon.

"Oh, yeah." Shantel buried her face in her favorite horse's mane and tried to hide her pain. As if she knew something was wrong, Lady whinnied.

She fisted away a tear, angry at herself for allowing the pointless indulgence when tears wouldn't change things. Because there were no *if only*s in life. There was only the certainty you had to deal with the hand you were dealt and face the consequences no matter how bleak they sometimes seemed.

She'd done that when her mother had died. Had learned to deal with the pain and push it all down inside and move on.

"Don't try and fool me, young lady." Her father pulled her away from the horse and into his arms. "I know when you're upset."

"Daddy…you don't have to do this." Shantel tried to move away, but he held on tighter until eventually she gave up and accepted the hug. And when she did, the floodgates opened.

"That's right, Buttercup. Let it all out," her father said soothingly.

And so Shantel bawled right there in the middle of the stables, where any of the stable hands could see her falling apart. When she was done, one side of her father's shirt was soaked with her tears, but he didn't care. He led her out of the stables and to the farmhouse. When they made it to the porch, he sat Shantel in one of the rocking chairs he and her mother had used frequently and walked inside.

Shantel didn't know how long she sat there looking out over the farm's beautiful landscape, but eventually he returned carrying a teacup and saucer. "For you, baby girl," her father said. "Chamomile and honey."

"Thanks, Daddy."

"You know, I haven't see you cry like that, well, since the day I told you about your mother," he said, glancing in her direction. "After that, you clammed up and never really spoke about your feelings other than you wanted to be a psychiatrist to help other people with mental illness."

"I couldn't, Daddy." When he peered at her strangely,

she continued. "Cry, that is. It wasn't going to change anything. It wasn't going to bring her back. I felt like I failed Mama. I didn't see the signs of how unhappy she was. So unhappy she took her own life with no thought to those she would leave behind, her children who needed her desperately."

"I'm so sorry, Shantel. I had no idea you were harboring guilt over your mother's suicide. You must know it wasn't your fault."

Shantel shook her head. "I should have done more."

"You were eighteen and had gone off to college. What more could you do?"

"I don't know. Something." Her voice rose. "*Anything* to prevent her from taking her own life."

"She was sick, Shantel. You know this. You've studied this. Sometimes even with the best therapy you can't stop someone if they're determined to die."

"But we needed her," Shantel cried, tears once again sliding down her cheeks. "*I* still need her."

"Oh, Shantel." He pulled her into the comfort and safety of his arms. "You should have told me you had these feelings long ago. We could have worked through them."

"I've tried, Daddy. I went to therapy. I know the drill. But some wounds never really heal."

"I hope you know I did all I could for your mother," he said when she settled down again in the rocker. "She was in therapy and on meds. But she had a troubled past when we met and I thought I could save her. Take her away from the past hurts. I brought her here, but it didn't work. She was fundamentally unhappy and it seemed the more children we had, the worse she became. She was overwhelmed taking care of you all. Often I had to step in and take care of you kids."

Shantel frowned. "I had no idea things were so bad."

"Because I wanted to preserve your mother's image in your eyes. I made sure you only saw her when she was at her best, but it wasn't easy keeping up the pretense. Sometimes I thought about putting her away in an institution somewhere, but I just couldn't do it. I couldn't take away her freedom. So instead, she lived her years out here with me on the farm and I did my best. I know it wasn't perfect, but I tried. I'm sorry I failed you."

"Oh, Daddy, no!" Shantel reached for his hands. "It's not your fault. It's not mine either. And I think I'm finally starting to see that."

"I'm so glad, Buttercup. Because you and your brothers mean the world to me and I only want you to be happy."

"I want to be happy too."

"So, will you tell me what's happened between you and Roman?"

Shantel shook her head. Their falling out was between them and she didn't want to color her father's image of Roman in his mind. Even now, she was protecting him when he couldn't care less about her. "No, not really. Give me time to sort through this, if that's okay?"

"Absolutely." Her father patted her knee. "I'm here when you need me. And if it's all the same to you, I'm going to check on Lady. I didn't like the noise she made earlier."

Shantel smiled. "Thanks, Daddy, for looking after Lady and for always looking after me."

Twenty-One

Roman was heading to his car in the executive parking lot on his way to find Shantel when he ran into Josiah. His father's driver was pulling the Bentley up to the curb as Roman was exiting.

"Going somewhere?" Josiah asked.

"Yeah, I am." Roman didn't elaborate and continued to his car. He hadn't spoken to his old man since the night of the party. He'd been livid with him for how he'd spoken about Shantel when she'd been nothing but gracious.

"Wait!" Josiah demanded. "You're leaving? Just like that? You're not going to gloat about signing Curtis?"

"Why would I?" Roman asked, cocking his head to one side. "I told you I would sign him and I did. With Shantel's help."

"Oh, I get it, you're upset about what I said about your fiancée," his father replied.

"What the hell do you think?" Roman responded. He tried to calm himself because he was talking to his father, the man he loved and had once wanted to emulate. But not now. He never wanted to be so money- and power-hungry that he lost human decency like his dad.

"Listen, I know I may have come across a little harsh on Saturday, but I was trying to light a fire under you and it worked. You sealed the deal."

"No thanks to you," Roman said. "As I told you that night and I'll tell you again, I'm done with kowtowing to you. I've done everything you've ever asked of me and then some and still you continue to push."

"Because you have that same fire in your belly like I do," Josiah said. "That same killer instinct. I've always known and I've helped you hone it so when you take over, no one can touch you."

"Well, someone has touched me, Dad," Roman responded. "Shantel has touched me in ways I've never imagined, and I may have lost her because I failed to stand up to you. Failed to tell you what a beautiful, amazing, smart and caring lady she is. Because I didn't fight for her. But I'm going to do that now, which is why I'm stepping down as COO."

"No!" his father shouted. "You can't do that. You're my heir. You're the next in line. I've been grooming you for years."

"But you don't respect me."

"Oh, but I do," his father said, walking toward him and clasping Roman's shoulder. "Of all my sons, you've had the most potential in business. Julian has his medicine and Xavier, up until two years ago, had his football. But you, you have always been the apple of my eye. *My son!*"

"This is all a little too late, Dad," Roman said, wrenching himself out of his father's grasp. "I needed to have heard all this a long time ago. And it's too late. I have to go and find Shantel. Make this right somehow. Make her see that she means more to me than anything." He turned and walked to the driver's side of his Maserati Levante.

"More than the Atlanta Cougars?"

Roman glanced across the top of the car. "Yes."

His father sighed. "You must love her a great deal if you're willing to give up your birthright."

"I do," Roman responded. "And I'm going to get her back." Which was why he was willing to leave it all in his rearview for the love of one woman. His woman.

"I don't know, Charlene, my cake looks nothing like yours," Shantel said, gazing at her lopsided German chocolate cake sitting on the counter that evening at the Wilson family home.

Her sister-in-law had come over because Shantel was craving one of her chocolate cakes. When she arrived, Charlene had all the makings for several cakes along with her nephew in a baby carrier. Shantel had always wanted to learn how to bake so she'd insisted on trying, but her cake was an epic failure while Charlene's was perfectly round and symmetrical.

"You'll get it," Charlene said. "Sometimes baking isn't for everyone. You're a fabulous cook, while I burn everything I touch. It's why your brother cooks all the time. So don't sweat the small stuff. Roman isn't marrying you for your baking."

"Speaking of Roman…" Shantel went to the carrier and pulled her nephew out. She inhaled deeply. Christopher smelled of baby powder and she loved his big fat cheeks. "We're sort of on a break for a moment."

"Break?" Charlene repeated. "What do you mean? Your wedding is in a few days. I should have known something was up when you arrived less than a week before your wedding, claiming you wanted some family time. I thought maybe you had cold feet."

"It's more than cold feet," Shantel said. "I don't know if Roman is the man I thought he was."

"Why would you say that?"

"His values are wrong," she replied. "He's all about money and power and prestige. I couldn't care less about those things. I want to be happy. Have a healthy baby. A loving husband. Is that too much to ask?"

"It isn't," a deep male voice said from behind her.

Shantel swallowed hard, her heart pounding fast in her chest when she heard Roman's voice. He was in her safe haven. She turned to face him.

"I want you to be happy too," Roman said, "and I think you can be, with me and our baby."

"Well, that's my cue to leave." Charlene came to Shantel and pulled her nephew out of her arms. "I hope to see you both—" she glanced in Roman's direction "—at the wedding." She bundled the baby into the carrier and within seconds she was out the door, leaving Shantel and Roman alone in the kitchen.

"What are you doing here?" Shantel asked.

"Isn't it obvious? I'm here to win you back. I went to

your office, your house, but you weren't there. I came to tell you I was a complete idiot for valuing all those things you mentioned above you. Above us."

Shantel turned away. "There is no us, Roman. You saw to that on Saturday night."

She heard his footsteps and then he was spinning her around. "I know I made a mistake. A big one, Shantel, but I'm asking you for another chance."

"So, what? You can weave a magic spell around me so I walk down the aisle?" Shantel asked. "Come on. I have more self-respect than that." She had already become a cliché, falling for someone who was never going to love her back. Now it was up to Shantel to hold her head up high and get on with her life.

"I'm asking you to listen. Not just with your head, but with your heart," Roman implored. "Please."

"All right." Shantel would hear him out but only this once. She led him into her father's study so they would have no interruptions. "Say what you have to say and then leave me in peace."

"I'm sorry to tell you, sweetheart, but that isn't going to happen."

Shantel was afraid she'd weaken, because hadn't he always had that effect on her? From the moment they'd met, she hadn't been able to see anyone else but him. And Shantel feared she never would.

The drive to McDonough from Atlanta had been snarled and riddled with traffic, and Roman's nerves had become more and more frayed as an unfamiliar thought nagged at him. *What if Shantel won't forgive me?* She had every right to be upset with him, but he'd come here with his hat in his hand, asking for another chance, and he wasn't leaving until she heard him out.

"Are we back to *that* Roman?" Shantel shot back. "The one who demands and orders me around? Because if so, you can get in your Maserati and drive back to Atlanta."

She was right. Being hard-nosed wasn't going to get him on her good side. He had to make her realize *why* he'd come here.

"Well?" She looked at him, then pointedly glanced down at her watch. "I don't have all night."

Roman sucked in a deep breath and realized he was nervous. It wasn't going to be easy—he would have to do something he'd never done before. Something he'd shied away from his whole life. He was going to have to spill his guts even though there was no guarantee Shantel would accept him or what he had to say. It might be too late.

He looked into her wary eyes and his heart thudded. "First, I want to say how much I've missed you these last few days. It's been agony without you."

"And second?"

"I need to ask for your forgiveness. I should have stood up to my father when he said all those horrible things about you, but instead I acted like the scared little boy I've always been around Josiah. I didn't defend you. I didn't stand up to him and tell him how strong, kind, caring, thoughtful, beautiful and extremely passionate you are." At her blush, he continued, "I love you, Shantel. No one has ever made me feel the way you do. I feel complete, as if I've found the missing piece I never knew I needed. I want to spend the rest of my life with you and our baby."

Shantel took a step back. "You're only saying these things because you know it's what I want to hear. You don't really want me. You want the baby." She patted her stomach. "And you're being cruel by saying these things. Why can't you just let me go?"

He shook his head. "That's not true. I want *you*, Shantel. And only you. You're smart and funny and sassy and I love every part of you."

Shantel felt a lump forming in her throat and she blinked her eyes rapidly to keep from tearing up. "I don't know if I can believe you, Roman."

"But you want to," he said. "I can see it in your eyes because it's in your nature to believe the best of people, to forgive. And I don't know what happened to your mom, but I'm here to tell you that you are worthy of love. I love you and I want to be with you. I'll never leave you, Shantel."

"I'm scared." Hot tears sprang to her eyes, and this time Shantel couldn't seem to stop them from falling. "Really scared that this is all a dream and I'm going to wake up any minute."

"Sweetheart." Roman came toward her and eased her into his arms. "It's not a dream. It's real. I love you. And to prove it, I told my father I'm giving it all up. I don't need or want to run the Atlanta Cougars if I'm going to wind up like him, hung up on money and power."

"Oh, Roman." Shantel reached out and caressed his cheek. "You don't have to give up everything to prove you love me."

He halted her protest by placing his finger on her lips. “But I will, because that’s how much you mean to me. Besides, I have my own money. I don’t need to run the franchise.”

“But you want to.”

“I won’t lie. I’ve worked my entire life towards that goal, but there’s no life for me without *you* in it. With you by my side, I can conquer the world. And speaking of that, I signed Curtis.”

“You did!” She threw her arms around Roman, so full of joy for him. “That’s wonderful. But it’s also why you can’t leave. You gave Tim your word that you would take care of his son.”

“But I have to take care of you and our baby first.” He placed his palm over the small swell of her stomach.

“I love you, Roman, but you don’t have to choose one or the other. You can have us both.”

“I can?” He sounded incredulous.

She nodded through her tears. “Yes, because that’s what you do for someone you love. You make sacrifices. And Roman, I love you with all my heart. I think I have since I saw you standing across from me in the ballroom that night at the Bachelor Auction. And I’ve been scared too, scared of being left alone. My mother’s suicide messed with my head, made me think I was unlovable, and Bobby leaving after her death cemented that notion.”

“Shantel, why have you never told me this before?”

She shrugged. “It’s been too difficult to talk about these things. It was only recently that my Dad and I talked, *really talked* about my mother and her mental illness. He helped me see it wasn’t my fault.”

"Of course it wasn't." Roman stroked her cheek. "She was sick, but you weren't to blame. Is this why you clammed up when I suggested having more children?"

Shantel nodded. "I was afraid. What if it's genetic?"

"You can't think the worst, sweetheart. And no matter what happens, I love you. If you don't want any more children, this one—" he rubbed her belly "—will be our only child."

"No." Shantel shook her head. "I love you, Roman, and I want a whole brood of your babies."

"You do?"

Tears slid down her cheeks because he sounded so unsure. "Oh, yes, you woke me out of the fog. I've barely been living, Roman, but that night you sparked me to life, and I never want that light to go out."

"It was the same for me," Roman said, wiping away her tears. "Seeing you at the art gallery was like a thunderbolt to my system. I'd tried to forget you, but I couldn't. I'm so thankful fate brought you back into my life and gave me a do-over. And I don't want to waste a single minute of our second chance. So, Shantel." He dropped to his knees in front of her. "Will you marry me?"

Shantel laughed through her tears. "Get up, silly. We're already engaged."

"Yeah, we are." He took a shuddering breath. "But the first time I didn't do it right. This time, I'm kneeling before you, telling you that you're my heart's desire and I want you to be mine and I want to be yours for the rest of our lives. So if you'll have me, Shantel, I'd like for you to be my wife."

Her eyes were so rich and full of emotion, Roman could scarcely breathe as he waited for her response.

"Yes. Yes!" She wound her arms around his neck, pulled him to his feet and kissed him. Her kiss was tender and brought with it a lightness and brightness Roman hadn't known was missing from his life.

He returned the kiss, murmuring sweet words to her as she pressed herself against him. He swept her up, carrying her upstairs to her former bedroom, where he lay down beside her, cradling her, kissing her until eventually their kisses grew passionate and they made sweet love.

Shantel was everything he'd ever wanted. She was the woman he loved. And now she would always be his. Now and forever.

Epilogue

"As much as I loved seeing you walk down the aisle to me," Roman said, a week later at the Pristine Chapel in Jonesboro about twenty-five miles outside Atlanta, "I'm happy the wedding is over."

He and Shantel had married as planned, earlier that day inside a black gazebo on the water, surrounded by manicured lawns and lush trees. The Pristine Chapel offered them a large event space to hold all their hundred plus guests. The wedding planner had outdonc herself with the decor and bountiful floral arrangements. All of the Locketts were there, including his father, who'd apologized to Shantel the minute she returned to Atlanta. He'd had to, otherwise Roman would have never forgiven him. But in the end, Roman had forgiven his father because his heart held too much love for Shantel not to make peace with his family. But the Wilsons' contingent made up most of the guest list.

Shantel looped her arms around his neck. "Didn't you like seeing me in my wedding dress?"

Roman stepped back to look at his beautiful wife in the glittery tulle and strapless lace mermaid gown but kept his arms around her waist. "You were beautiful. The most beautiful bride in the world, and I couldn't tear my eyes away from you."

"Oh, you know the right things to say, Mr. Lockett."

"Then how about this? I can't wait to see you out of this wedding dress," he said with a wicked glint in his eye.

"You're going to have to work for it," Shantel said. "It took Vanessa half an hour to button each of those pearl buttons." Her best friend had stood up as her maid of honor after she'd made Roman promise to always love and care for Shantel at the rehearsal dinner the night before.

Roman knew he'd have no problem with that vow. He'd also had a serious talk with his father, which included an apology to Shantel for his abysmal behavior and thanking her for helping to ink the deal with Curtis. They'd also established the conditions for Roman's return to the company. His father would have to take a step back as general manager and give Roman free rein to run the Atlanta Cougars as he saw fit. His father hadn't liked it, but because their mother was ready to travel and see the world, Josiah had relented, and he was happy to have Roman back in the fold.

Roman was happier than he'd ever been. He had his company, but most of all he had a beautiful bride he was dying to get out of her wedding dress. Adeptly he unbuttoned the costly gown until it pooled around Shantel's feet, leaving her in nothing but her underwear and a pair of very high white stilettos.

He sucked in a deep breath as he admired her beautiful body that would soon grow big with his child. He couldn't wait for the new addition to their family, a little baby with Shantel's big brown eyes and her big smile. He moved over her then and looked down at her. "Thank you."

"For?"

"For loving me," Roman said. Meeting Shantel had changed his life, and he would always be thankful she'd taken a chance and been the high bidder on his heart.

* * * * *

If you loved Roman and Shantel,
you won't want to miss
Julian and Elyse's story
as the Locketts of Tuxedo Park series
by Yahrah St. John
continues!
Available August 2021
from Harlequin Desire.

COMING NEXT MONTH FROM

HARLEQUIN

DESIRE

Available May 11, 2021

#2803 THE TROUBLE WITH BAD BOYS
Texas Cattleman's Club: Heir Apparent
by Katherine Garbera
Landing bad boy influencer Zach Benning to promote Royal's biggest soiree is a highlight for hardworking Lila Jones. And the event's marketing isn't all that's made over! Lila's sexy new look sets their relationship on fire... Will it burn hot enough to last?

#2804 SECOND CHANCE COUNTRY
Dynasties: Beaumont Bay • by Jessica Lemmon
Country music star Cash Sutherland hasn't seen Presley Cole since he broke her heart. Now a journalist, she's back in his life and determined to get answers he doesn't want to give. Will their renewed passion distract her from the truth?

#2805 SEDUCTION, SOUTHERN STYLE
Sweet Tea and Scandal • by Cat Schield
When Sienna Burns gets close to CEO Ethan Watts to help her adopted sister, she's disarmed by his Southern charm, sex appeal...and insistence on questioning her intentions. Now their explosive chemistry has created divided loyalties that may derail all her plans...

#2806 THE LAST LITTLE SECRET
Sin City Secrets • by Zuri Day
It's strictly business when real estate developer Nick Breedlove hires interior designer—and former lover—Samantha Price for his new project. Sparks fly again, but Samantha is hiding a secret. And when he learns the truth about her son, she may lose him forever...

#2807 THE REBEL HEIR
by Niobia Bryant
Handsome restaurant heir Coleman Cress has always been rebellious—in business and in relationships. Sharing a secret no-strings affair with confident Cress family chef Jillian Rossi is no different. But when lust becomes something more, can their relationship survive meddling exes and family drama?

#2808 HOLLYWOOD EX FACTOR
LA Women • by Sheri WhiteFeather
Security specialist Zeke Mitchell was never interested in the spotlight. When his wife, Margot Jensen, returns to acting, their marriage ends...but the attraction doesn't. As things heat up, are the problems of their past too big to overlook?

SPECIAL EXCERPT FROM

HARLEQUIN

DESIRE

Country music star Cash Sutherland hasn't seen Presley Cole since he broke her heart. Now a journalist, she's back in his life and determined to get answers he doesn't want to give. Will their renewed passion distract her from the truth?

Read on for a sneak peek at
Second Chance Love Song
by Jessica Lemmon.

"Did you expect me to sleep in here with you?"

And there it was. The line that he hadn't thought to draw but now was obvious he'd need to draw.

He eased back on the bed, shoved a pillow behind his back and curled her into his side. Arranging the blankets over both of them, he leaned over and kissed her wild hair, smiling against it when he thought about the tangles she'd have to comb out later. He hoped she thought of why they were there when she did.

"We should talk about that, yeah?" he asked rhetorically. He felt her stiffen in his arms. "I want you here, Pres. In this bed. Naked in my arms. I want you on my dock, driving me wild in that tiny pink bikini. But we should be clear about what this is…and what it's not."

She shifted and looked up at him, her blue eyes wide and innocent, her lips pursed gently. "What it's not."

"Yeah, honey," he continued, gentler than before. "What it's not."

"You mean…" She licked those pink lips and rested a hand tenderly on his chest. "You mean you aren't going to marry me and make an honest woman out of me after that?"

Cash's face broadcasted myriad emotions. From what Presley could see, they ranged from regret to nervousness to confusion and finally to what she could only describe as "oh, shit." That was when she decided to let him off the hook.

Chuckling, she shoved away from him, still holding the sheet to her chest. "God, your face! I'm kidding. Cash, honestly."

He blinked, held that confused expression a few moments longer and then gave her a very unsure half smile. "I knew that."

"I'm not the girl you left at Florida State," she told him. "I grew up, too, you know. I learned how the world worked. I experienced life beyond the bubble I lived in."

She took his hand and laced their fingers together. She still cared about him, so much. After that, she cared more than before. But she also wasn't so foolish to believe that sex—even earth-shattering sex—had the power to change the past. The past was him promising to wait for her and then leaving and never looking back.

"That was really fun," she continued. "I had a great time. You looked like you had a great time. I'm looking forward to doing it again if you're up to the task."

SPECIAL EXCERPT FROM

Here's a special sneak peek at
Follow Your Heart,
the fourth book in the Catalina Cove series from
New York Times *bestselling author Brenda Jackson.*

Coming soon from HQN Books!

Victoria knocked on the door to her great-grandmother's suite.

"Come in."

Opening the door, Victoria found her great-grandmother sitting in her favorite chair, knitting. Felicia Laverne Madaris had taught Victoria to knit when she'd been eight, and for her to still be able to use her hands to knit the way she did was amazing.

"Hello, Mama Laverne," Victoria said, leaning down to place a kiss on the older woman's cheek.

"And hello to you, Victoria."

Her great-grandmother was wearing a pretty floral dress with her signature pearls around her neck. Perched on her nose was a pair of reading glasses. While growing up, Victoria had thought her great-grandmother was one of the most stylish women she knew. She still thought so.

"You look pretty today, Mama Laverne."

PHBJEXP0421

“Thank you. And so do you. Would you like some Madaris tea?” Mama Laverne asked, placing her knitting aside and removing her reading glasses.

Victoria loved the Madaris tea. The recipe was known only to certain Madaris family members. “Yes. You want me to pour?” Victoria asked.

“That will be fine, dear.”

After pouring them both cups of tea, Victoria noticed Mama Laverne studying her intently. She knew there was a reason for her doing so, and she figured if she was patient, her great-grandmother would tell her what was on her mind.

After taking a couple sips of tea, Mama Laverne said, “I’m sure you know why I wanted to meet with you.”

Victoria nodded. “Yes, I do have a good idea.”

Mama Laverne took another sip of tea. “I know some of you merely see me as a meddling old woman, intent on destroying your lives. But as you can see, I haven’t steered anyone wrong yet.”

Victoria chuckled. “No, you haven’t. Nolan is happy with Ivy, Lee is happy with Carly, Reese is happy with Kenna, Luke is happy with Mac… Need I go on?”

Follow Your Heart *by Brenda Jackson*

HQNBooks.com

PHBJEXP0421